Magic
Below

Bewitched in Oz is published by Stone Arch Books
A Capstone imprint
1710 Roe Crest Drive
North Mankato, Minnesota 56003
www.mycapstone.com

Library of Congress Cataloging-in-Publication Data

Burns, Laura J., author.
Magic below / by Laura J. Burns.
pages cm. -- (Bewitched in Oz ; 2)

Summary: Zerie has learned that the real threat to Oz is Glinda the "Good" and her alliance with the Nome King, and now Ozma has magically transformed her into a mermaid and asked her to infiltrate Glinda's underwater palace, and free the Glass Cat and her friend, Brink—and she still is not completely sure who she can trust.

ISBN 978-1-62370-613-5 (paper over board) — ISBN 978-1-4965-2603-8 (library binding) — ISBN 978-1-4965-2604-5 (ebook pdf)

1. Oz (Imaginary place)--Juvenile fiction. 2. Magic--Juvenile fiction. 3. Mermaids--Juvenile fiction. 4. Trust--Juvenile fiction. 5. Adventure stories. [1. Fantasy. 2. Magic--Fiction. 3. Characters in literature--Fiction. 4. Mermaids--Fiction. 5. Friendship--Fiction. 6. Adventure and adventurers--Fiction.] I. Title.

PZ7.B937367Mag 2016
813.6--dc23
[Fic]
                           2015026795

Designer: Kay Fraser

Printed in China.
092015   009225S16

Magic Below

by Laura J. Burns

cover illustration by Liam Peters

Stone Arch Books
A casptone imprint

.1.

Darkness.

That's all there was. Darkness so profound that he couldn't see his hand an inch from his face. He might be in a tiny box or in a huge cavern. There was no way to tell. His breath was loud in his ears, and his heart pounded so hard that it actually hurt.

I have to calm down, Brink Springer thought. *My fear is making me imagine things. It can't really be this dark. I have to let my eyes adjust.*

He stared into the blackness, trying to slow his heartbeat, staying focused on taking deep breaths. It was still dark.

Brink closed his eyes, then opened them again.

Still dark. Pitch-black.

Maybe it's an illusion, he thought. Brink's magical talent was making illusions, and he'd gotten pretty good at it during the past week as he traveled through the Land of Oz.

He'd even begun to think that he could see through other people's illusions, too. But if this was one, he couldn't tell. *If not an illusion, then what?* he wondered.

No regular night could be like this, completely without light. Normally there were stars and the moon, but not tonight. It was simply never this black. It never had been in Brink's sixteen years of life. Somewhere, there had to be a torch or a candle. Somewhere, a tiny bit of light had to reach him . . . if everything was normal. But nothing had been normal since he had reached Glinda the Good's Palace. The golden bridge across the raging river had looked broken to his friends, but Brink could see it. He'd run over the delicate span to the gates of the famous sorceress's castle, hoping to prove to his friends that the broken bridge was only an illusion. He'd expected them to see him safe on the other side and to follow him. But that hadn't happened.

Brink's pulse sped up again as he thought of Zerie

Greenapple, her eyes going wide with terror as a Winged Monkey scooped her up into the air. Another Monkey had taken Vashti Weaver, and all Brink could do was watch helplessly from the bridge as his two friends were carried off by the agents of Princess Ozma to their giant airship hovering overhead. Why hadn't the Monkeys taken him, too?

Brink had turned to the golden doors of Glinda's Palace, banging on them with both fists. He'd known his only chance was to get the attention of the great sorceress, to beg for her help. It was the reason he, Zerie, and Vashti had traveled so far from their home in the north of Quadling Country. Glinda was the only one with the power to oppose Princess Ozma and her ban on magic in the Land of Oz.

The golden gates had swung open, and Brink saw her: Glinda, as beautiful as all the old tales had said, with long red hair, piercing blue eyes, and a gown of sparkling white so bright it almost hurt to look at.

"Help!" Brink had cried, falling to his knees in front of her. "Ozma has taken my friends."

Glinda had smiled at him. Smiled, and raised her hand . . .

Then there had been a loud sound, like a clap of

thunder, and the next thing he knew, it was dark, and he was alone.

Brink laid his hand on the ground, which felt cold and rough beneath his palm. He didn't know if he had seen Glinda a few seconds ago or a few days ago. The darkness had come as such a shock that he wasn't sure if he'd lost consciousness or if he'd simply been transported here by magic. He felt sure of only one thing, and that was Glinda herself.

She'd smiled at him, and it hadn't been a friendly smile. It had been a triumphant smile. A mocking smile. A cruel smile.

Glinda wasn't Good. Glinda was evil.

Brink drew in a breath and concentrated on the darkness. His eyes weren't adjusting to it the way they normally would. He needed light. Brink thought about the hurricane lamp he kept on his bedside table at home and wondered if he could create an illusion of light. He imagined himself sitting in bed, glancing over at the lamp as he reached to turn it off. He did this every single night, so the lamp was as familiar to him as his red wooden nightstand, his well-worn blanket, and the smell of oil drifting up from the workroom where his dad and his older brother, Ned, built their clockwork machines. Brink had never spent much time staring at his hurricane lamp, but now he conjured the image in his mind and studied the rounded glass that made up the base, the copper dial that controlled the wick, the reddish oil that filled it, the flame that glowed bright and cheerful in the top. The flame. Yellow with a hint of blue at the wick. Magnified by the glass that surrounded it, warming the air. Lighting the room. Brink could picture the flame perfectly, could feel the image of it struggling to push its way out of him and form in the empty air. An illusion that looked absolutely real. He did it all the time.

But this time nothing happened.

Brink sighed. It was no use. He couldn't make an illusion. His friend the Glass Cat had said that Glinda's Palace was protected by such a strong enchantment that no magic would work there other than her own. Did that mean he was still in Glinda's Palace?

Slowly, Brink lay down on the cold, rough floor. He concentrated on the space around him. Was he in a room? He couldn't sense any walls. Could he be under a spell, one that made him blind? Could he be in some sort of underground pit, where no light reached him?

The ground beneath him felt like rock. Brink turned

on his side and pressed his cheek against it. Somehow, the hardness of it comforted him. He couldn't see a thing, but he could feel this solid surface. He closed his eyes and tried to think of home. His father tinkering with a clockwork. His brother sitting on the porch. Brink's pounding heart slowed a little, and he felt his shoulders relax.

A whirring sound.

Brink caught his breath, surprised. He hadn't noticed it before, but now that he had calmed down, he heard a sound clearly. Or rather, he *felt* a sound. His whole body vibrated with it. The entire floor vibrated, in fact.

He sat up, then stood up. The sound was quieter, and the vibration was gone.

Brink eased himself back down to the floor, stretching his body out on the cold, hard rock. The sound hummed loudly in his ear, and his body vibrated again.

It's moving, Brink realized with a shock. *The ground is moving.*

But how could that be? If he were in an underground pit, the ground wouldn't move. If he were in a normal room, it wouldn't be so dark.

"It must be an enchantment," he said aloud. It was

comforting to hear a voice, even if it was only his own. "I'm in one of Ozma's airships, and they've put a spell on me to blind me." It was the only explanation. The malevolent way Glinda had smiled at him made it clear that she was no better than Princess Ozma. She had most likely been in league with Ozma right from the moment the princess had banned magic, so she had zapped him up here and placed a magical blindfold on his eyes. He was in the airship, on his way to the Emerald City to stand before Ozma. The ruler of Oz would accuse him of using his magic, and then she would make him step into the Forbidden Fountain, where the Water of Oblivion would erase his memories and his magical talent.

Still, Brink felt happy.

If he was in the airship, he might be with Zerie and Vashti. The Monkeys had been taking them to the Forbidden Fountain, and there was no reason to think that Glinda hadn't sent Brink along with them. Maybe his friends were blinded, too, to keep them from fighting their captors.

"Zerie?" he called. "Are you here? Can you hear me?" He waited for a few seconds. "Vashti? It's me, it's Brink. Are you here?"

There was no answer.

Brink sighed. Maybe the spell had blocked his hearing as well as his sight. But no—he could hear his own voice and he could hear that vibration. Could Zerie and Vashti be under some kind of spell, too? Or maybe they were all being held in separate rooms.

Frustrated, he stood up and stuck his hands out in front of him. It was a little scary to walk forward when he couldn't see a thing, but he did it anyway. He had to know what was around him. After about six paces, his fingers hit a wall. It felt cold and rough, just like the floor. Brink kept one hand on the wall and walked beside it until he suddenly hit another wall, right in front of his face.

"Ouch," Brink murmured, shaking his head at his own thoughtlessness. He began walking again, one hand trailing the new wall, the other hand out in front of him. This time, when he reached the corner, he'd feel it before he walked into it.

He'd counted fifteen paces along the first wall. This wall was longer. He counted twenty paces. Then thirty. Then forty. When he reached fifty paces, he slowed down. How could the room possibly be so large? He stopped walking.

The wall beneath his fingers kept moving.

Brink stood still, staring into the blackness. The wall was moving? How? Why? Where was he?

"That's what the sound is, and the vibration," he said out loud. "It's movement." But how did that fit in with being on an airship? The wall wouldn't move on an airship—the whole ship would move. So if not on the ship with the Winged Monkeys, where was he? Thoughts whirled around in Brink's head, filling him with frustration. He shut his eyes and pressed his hands against them, just to see the stars against his eyelids. The darkness was making him crazy.

When he opened his eyes again, it was gray.

Brink caught his breath, surprised. Was he imagining it? The change was so slight that he wasn't sure it was real. He held his hand right in front of his face. This time he thought he could make out its shape. At least, there seemed to be a deeper sort of blackness where his hand should've been. As he watched, it grew clearer. He wiggled his fingers and saw movement.

His heart pounded. Was the blindness wearing off? Or the enchantment? Did it mean that Glinda had reversed her spell? Were they nearing the Emerald City? Maybe Glinda would lift the blindness so that he could look Ozma in the eye before she sentenced him to the Forbidden Fountain. A chill ran through Brink at the thought. He and Zerie and Vashti had talked about losing their magical talents in the Water of Oblivion. Zerie had always said it would be like losing a part of herself, and Brink felt the same way. He wouldn't be himself if he couldn't make illusions.

He could see more now. The darkness lifted more with each passing second.

Zerie and Vashti's other best friend, Tabitha, had been obsessed with old tales of the heroes of Oz—Ozma and Dorothy of Kansas, Glinda and the Wizard. Tabitha had told them that the Water of Oblivion erased people's memories. Brink wasn't sure how exactly that would remove his magical talent, but now that he was facing it, he found it comforting that all his memories would be gone. If he couldn't remember his talent, maybe he wouldn't miss it.

He could forget the horror of killing a Kalidah, which he and Zerie had been forced to do in order to prevent the wild beast from tearing them apart on their long journey to Glinda's Palace. He could forget the stinging anger he'd felt when he realized that his older brother, Ned, had betrayed them, that he was working as a spy for Ozma. He could forget the fear coursing through his body as he watched Zerie being lifted into the sky by that Monkey.

But he'd also forget Zerie. Her green eyes, which could sparkle like an emerald when she was happy and could fill with a cold intensity when she was angry. Her fire-red hair that caught all the colors of a sunset. The warmth of her in his arms when she'd leaned against him for comfort after the Kalidah.

Just before they'd reached Glinda's Palace, Zerie had said she liked him. For years, Brink had had a crush on her, but she had obviously been interested in Ned. And now finally Zerie had noticed him. He didn't want to forget her. He didn't want to forget what they had together.

"Zerie has probably been forced into the Forbidden Fountain already," Brink muttered. "She's forgotten about me."

Brink could see his hand in front of his face clearly now, and the vibration seemed to be louder. He blinked, trying to adjust to the light. He'd never been enchanted before, but he was surprised by how un-magical this seemed. It felt more like stepping out of a dark room than snapping out of a sorceress's spell.

"To the back for your food!" a harsh voice called.

Brink spun around, shocked to hear a voice other than his own. The wall behind him was gone. Not entirely, but on the right side of the room, a shaft had opened from the ceiling to the floor, and orange light spilled through.

Brink shielded his eyes from the glare, looking down to keep from being dazzled. He'd been right—this room was made of rock. Dark reddish stone, he noticed. He glanced at the other three walls, which were all still in place. More of the same red stone. Meanwhile, the shaft in the fourth wall was growing wider, and now he could see through it.

There was something on the other side. Shadows moved against the light, and he heard a loud thrumming sound and a series of clangs and grunts and what sounded like more voices.

"To the back!" the voice yelled again.

As Brink watched, the shaft in the wall grew wider at a steady pace. The wall was moving, opening, like a sliding door leading to a different place. Now the opening was three feet wide, and he caught sight of a torch in a sconce on the wall outside his room. The wall continued sliding open, and a figure came into view—a man dressed in a dark pink soldier uniform. He stood before the moving wall, holding a wooden bowl and a small wooden cup. His eyes met Brink's and he bellowed, "To the back or no food!"

Startled, Brink realized that he'd been standing stock still, just gaping at the hole in the wall. He scuttled backward toward the red rock behind him, and the man leaned over and placed the bowl and the cup on the floor of Brink's room. After he put it down, the food moved past the soldier.

The wall isn't moving, Brink thought as he watched. *It's the whole room that's moving.*

Quickly, he looked back up at the opening in the wall. It was about eight feet wide now, and through it he could see a large room, lit with torches. The food man stood there on a red rock floor that was solid and still. Meanwhile, Brink's chamber glided past, stone sliding against stone. There were other people with the food man, some of them holding tall spears like the Winged Monkeys had. And in the center of their room was a tall, thick, round pole made of metal.

"Prisoner, stay back until you pass," the food man told him.

"What do you—?" Brink began, but the words died

on his lips. The opening was getting smaller again. Already it was only five feet wide. The food man wasn't in the middle anymore but off to the left. Brink looked at the metal pole. It was off to the left as well.

That was the axle. Brink had seen his father and Ned make a hundred different clockwork machines, so he understood how they worked even on a huge scale like this. His room was attached to that somehow, and it was spinning him around it in a circle. There weren't four walls to his room, there were only three. But when he glided past this opening, his chamber must go inside a cave or a tunnel. That's why the wall had seemed to move—because his whole room was moving past it.

Darkness crept slowly over his cell as the torchlit room grew smaller and smaller through the open wall. Brink felt despair stab through him as he realized that he was headed back into the utter blackness.

This is a dungeon, Brink thought, back in the dark. He'd been worried that he was going to Ozma, that he would be put into the Water of Oblivion.

This was worse.

.2.

"It's so dark," Zerie murmured.

"I know. I can hardly see you," her best friend Vashti replied, squeezing her hand as they followed Princess Ozma through a gently sloping tunnel.

"We'll be back up to the Royal Palace soon," Ozma told them, her voice as musical as a bell. "But I'll make a bit of light for you." She held out her hand, palm up, and a softly glowing orb of white light formed on top of it. The light glinted off of the dark green stone that formed the tunnel.

"We're under the Emerald City," Vashti whispered. "I still can't believe it! Will we get to see the Wizard again?"

Zerie smiled. Vashti had always loved stories about the Wizard. Of course, when they'd actually met him—less than an hour ago, though it seemed much longer—Oz's famous magician had sentenced them to the Forbidden Fountain as a punishment for using their magical talents. But they had emerged from the Water of Oblivion with their memories and talents intact. Princess Ozma had been waiting for them in the secret cavern beneath the fountain, and she'd explained everything: how her ban on magic had been meant to isolate those with talents so that she could find and protect them, how the Land of Oz was beset by a terrible enemy, and that the enemy was Ozma's old friend Glinda the Good.

But the Wizard hadn't been with Ozma in the cave. Only their friend Tabitha was there.

"Does the Wizard know? About Glinda, I mean?" Zerie asked. "He was nice to us when we arrived here, even though he was punishing us."

"He made an illusion to hide all the people watching us, so we wouldn't feel as bad about being . . . you know . . ." Vashti's voice trailed off.

"Paraded through the streets as prisoners and evildoers?" Tabitha finished for her. Tabitha had been the first one from their village arrested for doing magic, and she'd been here in Ozma's palace the longest. "He doesn't really approve of punishing witches and wizards. He's a wizard himself."

"But he doesn't know about Glinda, no," Princess Ozma put in sadly. "The Wizard is my dear friend, and I've told him that the Land of Oz is under attack. But I haven't said who our real enemy is. Ever since Glinda turned traitor, I'm afraid to trust anyone from my past. She was my closest advisor."

"You mean the Wizard could be a secret traitor, too?" Vashti asked, shocked.

"We can't trust anyone," Tabitha told her. "Only one another."

"We've always been able to do that." Zerie reached out and took Tabitha's hand, linking all three girls together in a chain. "I'm so happy to see you, Tabitha. We were worried about you."

Tabitha's pretty face lit up in a smile. "I was more worried about *you*, lost in the wild! Here I was, safe with Ozma, while you two were roaming through the Land of Oz on your own."

"Well, we had Brink with us," Vashti replied. "His talent was really helpful."

Just the mention of Brink's name made Zerie want to cry. He was Glinda's prisoner, and there was nothing she could do about it. "It wasn't only his talent that helped," she said. "It was him."

"Of course. That's what I meant!" Vashti said quickly. "The three of us made a great team. Friends are strongest together."

Zerie's grammy said that all the time, and she knew Vashti was trying to cheer her up by reciting it. But the truth was the three of them hadn't been a team. During the trek from their village to Glinda's Palace, she and Vashti had spent way too much time fighting and she and Brink had spent way too much time not admitting their feelings for each other. Yes, they had managed to work together when they were in danger, but Zerie felt ashamed of how much bickering they'd all done.

It seemed so silly now, compared to the terrible situation they were all in. For her whole life, Zerie had known Glinda the Good to be one of the most important and best people in the Land of Oz. The idea that she had turned on Oz's rightful ruler, Princess Ozma, was almost impossible to believe.

"Princess Ozma, are you *sure* that Glinda is the true

enemy?" Zerie asked. "Why would she try to take over Oz after so many years of being its protector?"

"I don't know why," Ozma replied. "But the Winged Monkeys have seen strangers near the borders of Winkie Country, and we think they are agents of the Nome King."

"The Nome King!" Vashti gasped.

"Oz's ancient enemy," Tabitha said. "I was shocked when Ozma told me. Of all people to be in league with, Glinda chose the worst."

Zerie shuddered. When she was little, her older sister, Zelzah, used to tell her stories about the Nome King. Tabitha had always come running to listen, too, since she'd loved the tales of old Oz even then. Zelzah had spoken of the many times the short-tempered king tried to conquer the Land of Oz, and of the way he raged whenever anyone mentioned the Emerald City to him. The Nome King felt that all gemstones under the earth belonged to him, since his kingdom was underground. In his mind, the emeralds were his, so the Emerald City should be his. He thought Ozma had stolen it from him . . . and he was willing to go to war to take it back.

"Glinda has always been a powerful sorceress. If

she wanted to rule Oz, why would she need the help of the Nome King?" Vashti asked.

Princess Ozma sighed. "I wish I understood that, or anything that's been happening. All I'm sure of is that my Monkeys and my other scouts see an army being raised. There have been rock men spotted rising from the Great Sandy Waste south of Glinda's Palace."

"I never really believed that part of the stories," Tabitha chimed in. "That the Nome King's servants were made of stone."

"Half made of stone," Vashti corrected her. "Half is man, half is stone."

"Zelzah said they were like statues come to life," Zerie added.

"All I can think is that Glinda has asked the Nome King for military help," Ozma said. "She can't conquer Oz through magic alone."

She stopped walking and held up her hand. The glowing orb illuminated a marvelous door made of gold, with a large emerald set in the center.

"You three know the truth, but the people of Oz do not," the princess said. "Although you could not see them, the citizens of the Emerald City watched you enter the Forbidden Fountain. As far as they know, you no longer have any magical talent nor any memory of being witches."

"Can we tell our families the truth?" Zerie asked, thinking of how sad Grammy would be to hear that she'd lost her talent.

"I don't think there will be time for you to return to your village, Zerie," Ozma said gently. "Our enemy is moving quickly, and we must do the same." She placed her free hand on the emerald, and the golden door swung silently open. On the other side was a hallway paved with green and gold tiles.

"Tonight you two will sleep safely here in my home," Princess Ozma said, smiling at Zerie and Vashti in turn. "It's been a very long and confusing day for you, and you need to rest."

Tabitha stepped forward. "I'll show you where your rooms are," she said. "Ozma has put your bedchambers on either side of mine."

Zerie turned to say goodbye to the princess, but Ozma had vanished.

Vashti blinked in surprise. "Did you make her disappear, Tabitha?"

Their friend laughed. "My talent has grown much stronger since the last time we saw one another, but

I'm not powerful enough to make a fairy princess vanish. Ozma has a magic all her own."

She led them down the hallway until they came to three arched silver doors inlaid with mother-of-pearl. Tabitha touched a door lightly, and it swung inward. "This is yours, Zerie."

Zerie stepped inside, hardly able to believe she was supposed to sleep here. The bedchamber was three times the size of her room at home, with high ceilings, a beautiful four-poster bed, and gorgeous draperies woven with gold and green thread. Zerie sighed.

"What's that for?" Tabitha asked teasingly. "Isn't it nice enough for you?"

"It's beautiful," Zerie told her. "But I'm too upset to sleep, even in a bed like this one."

"Me too," Vashti said. "Think about it: this time yesterday, we were in the Tilted Forest with Brink, trying to get to Glinda for help."

Zerie nodded, remembering what had happened in that sideways forest—how she and Brink had admitted that they liked each other, only to be interrupted by the Glass Cat. It was too distressing to think about Brink, and to wonder what he must be going through.

"What happened to the cat?" she asked, forcing her

mind away from Brink. "Did you see her at Glinda's Palace, Vash?"

"No." Vashti frowned. "She was always running off, though. I assumed she had done that again."

"The cat? What cat?" Tabitha asked.

"The Glass Cat. She helped us on our journey to Glinda," Zerie said. "I forgot you didn't know that. There's so much that we haven't talked about."

"The Glass Cat? Ozma's favorite pet?" Tabitha said, her hazel eyes sparkling. "She was in lots of the old Ozma stories!"

"Well, she wouldn't like you calling her a pet," Vashti said, smiling. "She is very prickly about that— she is her own creature and nobody else's."

"She disappeared right as we entered Glinda's lands. Remember? There was a pink haze around the castle, and as soon as we stepped into it, we noticed she was gone," Zerie said, frowning. "It's as if she led us there and then deserted us."

"But she deserted us all the time," Vashti said. "She ran away whenever there was danger."

"Maybe she sensed danger as the Winged Monkeys' airship approached," Tabitha said. "Although I suppose she would have told you about it before she ran."

"Not necessarily," Vashti replied. "She would've just thought we were stupid for not sensing the danger ourselves."

"The Glass Cat was the one who suggested that we go to Glinda for help in the first place," Zerie said slowly, thinking back to the night the Winged Monkeys had attacked their village. "She said Glinda was the only one who had the strength to fight Princess Ozma."

Vashti's eyebrows drew together in a frown. "Back then, we thought Ozma was the enemy. We thought the Monkeys had kidnapped Tabitha."

"They had, but it was only for show. They brought me here, the Wizard sentenced me, and I went into the Forbidden Fountain, just like you two," Tabitha said. "Ozma was waiting for me in the underground cavern, and she told me the truth."

"Right . . . but that means everything we thought we knew was backward," Vashti said. "The cat said Glinda could fight Ozma, and we thought that meant Glinda was good and Ozma was bad."

"But really it was the other way around," Zerie continued for her. "So the Glass Cat sent us to our enemy, not to our friend."

"You think the Glass Cat was working for Glinda?" Tabitha asked. "That she's an agent of the enemy?"

"The cat opposed Ozma's ban on magic. She said she hadn't seen Ozma since that law went into effect," Zerie said slowly. "If she truly hadn't seen Ozma, maybe she believed the ban was real, just like we did."

"Still, why send us straight to the enemy?" Vashti asked. "It's hard to be sure which side the Glass Cat was on."

"It's the same as with Ned Springer," Zerie said. "We didn't trust him when he found us in the Tilted Forest. We thought he was a spy for Ozma."

"Well, he was. He went through a lot of trouble to find you," Tabitha said. "We spent a lot of time together after I discovered the truth. Ned knew how important it was to me that you two were found safe."

"He was searching for us because Ozma wanted to bring us here safely, to ask us for help," Zerie said. "But we thought he was hunting us down to drag us off and take away our magical talents."

"It's not the same. You may not know which side the Glass Cat is on, but you do know about Ned. He's on our side," Tabitha said. "I'm sure of it."

Vashti shot Zerie a sideways look, raising her

eyebrows. Back in their village, she and Zerie had both had a crush on Ned, but he had liked Tabitha. From the way Tabitha was talking about him now, it seemed that maybe those feelings were mutual.

"If you say he is, you must be right. We thought Ned was an enemy, but he's a friend. We thought Glinda was a friend, but she's an enemy." Vashti shook her head. "I don't even know what to think about the Glass Cat."

"How can we be sure about any of this? How can we know who to trust?" Zerie asked.

Tabitha took Zerie's hands and smiled. "It's always been the three of us, from the first day we began practicing our talents together. We can trust one another."

Vashti nodded. "Definitely."

"I'll show you your room, Vashti. Zerie, try to get some sleep." Tabitha squeezed Zerie's hand and then headed for the door, Vashti following. It swung shut behind them without anyone even touching it.

"We can trust one another," Zerie murmured. But could they? Princess Ozma had trusted Glinda. They had been friends for years and years. Yet Glinda had still turned on the princess. How could she know for sure that her friends wouldn't turn on her?

Still, she and Vashti had been through so much together over the past week, surviving many dangers and strengthening their talents along the way. She knew in her heart that she could depend on her best friend. Just like she knew she could depend on Brink.

But he doesn't know he can depend on me, Zerie thought sadly. He'd been there every time she needed him, but she didn't feel like she had done the same for him. She'd refused to accept him at first, she'd spent all her time thinking about his brother, and then when she realized it was Brink she liked, she'd acted weird and jealous. She hadn't been a very good friend.

How must Brink have felt, watching the Winged Monkeys carry her off? What had happened to him when he met Glinda, if he met her? Had the great sorceress revealed her evil ways to him? Had she harmed him? Or had she convinced him that she was good, and that Ozma truly was the enemy?

Zerie walked to the tall window and peered out. A full moon hung, round and huge, in the sky. The Emerald City lay spread out around her, its yellow lights twinkling in the night sky, its green spires and battlements shining in the moonlight. It was even lovelier than she had dreamed it would be. But all she could think about was Glinda's Palace and what might be happening there.

A desperate thought seized her. She could leave right now and run to Glinda's Palace. The road of yellow brick led straight there, and with her magical talent for speeding things up, she could run the entire distance before anyone could catch her. Zerie took a deep breath, filled with confidence. When she, Brink, and Vashti had traveled to Glinda, they hadn't known the power of their talents. They had thought they needed to hide so they wouldn't be captured.

Now Zerie knew how strong she was. She knew exactly how to use her talent, and she knew she couldn't be stopped. She could speed straight to Glinda and rescue Brink. The great sorceress wouldn't even see her coming.

No matter how powerful you are, Glinda is more powerful, a little voice in her mind whispered.

Zerie ignored it. Brink was her friend, and he was in trouble. He needed her. She was going to save him— right now. She turned toward the bedchamber door . . . and gasped as it swung open.

In the doorway stood Brink's big brother. Ned Springer.

.3.

"Ned!" Zerie cried, stepping back from him. A rush of fear and anger filled her . . . and then vanished like a puff of smoke. The last time she had seen him, he had tried to trick her into coming with him. He pretended to be her friend, but he was actually one of Ozma's spies. And yet, Ozma was on their side.

Zerie shook her head, trying to clear away her confusion. "I'm sorry," she said with a sigh. "Ned, I was so used to thinking that Princess Ozma was my enemy. When I saw you, I forgot for a moment that if she's a friend, it means her spies are friends, too."

"I'd rather be called a scout than a spy," Ned said, his brown eyes twinkling. "But I forgive you, Zerie.

In fact, that's why I'm here. I hope I'm not bothering you?"

"No. I was just—" Zerie stopped. *Just quickly heading back to the place that your friends the Winged Monkeys saved me from, so I could somehow save your brother* didn't sound very sensible. She shrugged. "Come in."

"Thank you." Ned walked past her and stopped awkwardly in the middle of the room. "I wanted to apologize for the way I acted toward you, Zerie. I know you must've been frightened by all the Winged Monkeys and the airships. You probably thought I was a terrible person."

Zerie thought about the last time she'd seen Ned, in the Tilted Forest the day before she and her friends reached Glinda's Palace. He'd pretended to be searching for her, Vashti, and Brink. But as he spoke to them, the Winged Monkeys had appeared behind him, ready to attack.

Brink had been furious, accusing Ned of betraying him. Vashti had been thrown, too, since she still had a crush on Ned. And Zerie had also been some combination of shocked, scared, and angry on Brink's behalf. The truth was, she *had* thought Ned was terrible.

"I did," she admitted, her cheeks growing warm. It

was a strange thing to admit to someone, and she felt a little bad.

"I don't blame you," Ned replied gently. "All of Ozma's other servants were told that magical talents were dangerous, and that witches had to be captured and brought to the Emerald City for punishment. If I had let on that I knew you were really good, and that Ozma wanted your help, it could have been dangerous for you."

"How?" Zerie asked.

"Someone could have revealed your talent to our enemy, and she could have come after you," he told her. "Glinda has spies everywhere."

Zerie felt a pit form in her stomach. "That's what the Glass Cat said about Ozma."

"The Glass Cat? Is she a friend of yours?"

"I'm not sure. I thought she was, but maybe she was a spy herself." Zerie bit her lip. "It's so hard to know which side people are on. You were a spy, too, but you're on my side."

"Well, I'm not spying on you anymore. I'm here to help you and your friends. Vashti said she forgave me, and I hope you will, too."

"You spoke to Vashti already?"

"Yes, I went to her room and to Tabitha's, to make sure everyone was settled in for the night, and to apologize. Then I came to you." His eyes met hers, and he held her gaze for a long moment. "I wanted to save the best for last."

Zerie gaped at him. Was he flirting with her?

Ned took a step toward her, his expression intense. "Will you forgive me, Zerie? I'd be devastated if you were angry with me. You know how much I admire you."

He was definitely flirting with her.

"You told me you liked Tabitha," she blurted out.

Ned blinked in surprise. "Tabitha?"

"Back home, in my front parlor, you asked all about her," Zerie reminded him.

"Yes." Ned's easy smile returned. "I've spent a lot of time with Tabitha here in the Emerald City. She's a wonderful girl."

"She is," Zerie agreed. "And I get the feeling she thinks you're wonderful, too."

"Tabitha told me a lot of stories about the three of you. She says your talent is very impressive. Will you show me something?" he asked.

Zerie frowned. "Does Tabitha show you her talent?"

Ned shrugged. "I've never asked her to. I'm more interested in yours."

She hesitated. "I don't think I'm supposed to do magic in front of anybody. Princess Ozma wanted everyone to believe that the Water of Oblivion had removed our talents."

"Oh," Ned said, looking at his feet. "I understand. I was hoping . . . because we've known each other for so long . . . but I know you don't think I'm worth it."

"What do you mean?" Zerie asked.

"Back in the village, you always acted . . ." He ran a hand through his thick, dark hair. "Never mind."

"I acted like a fool," she finished for him. "Always finding an excuse to come by your house, like to ask you to fix our clockwork creatures."

Ned shook his head. "I never noticed that. I was happy to see you whenever you came over. But I thought . . . well, I thought maybe you looked down on me. And when I found out about your incredible talent, I understood why. I'm just a clockwork maker, and you're so powerful."

"What?" Zerie cried. "I didn't look down on you! I wanted to impress you!"

His face broke into a grin. "Well, you did." He

reached for her hands, holding them in both of his. "You really didn't think I was some kind of simpleton?"

"Of course not!"

"I'm glad. Because I've always liked you." Ned gazed into her eyes, and Zerie felt a wave of confusion. For so long, she'd had a crush on Ned. And now here he was, holding her hands, flirting with her, complimenting her. Her stomach filled with butterflies at the idea that Ned Springer could like her.

But something wasn't right.

Ned's eyes weren't quite like his brother's, and his hair was darker, and he was taller. Still, all Zerie could think about as she looked at him was how much he reminded her of Brink, and how worried she was about Brink.

"He doesn't even know you're good," she said suddenly.

Ned's eyebrows shot up. "Who?"

"Brink," Zerie said. "The last time he saw you, you were with the Monkeys, trying to capture us. Brink was so upset, because you were on the wrong side. You betrayed him. That's what he thought, anyway. And he probably still thinks that, in addition to whatever else he's going through."

She pulled her hands out of Ned's and turned away, all her fears for Brink returning.

"Zerie," Ned said from behind her. "We'll find him, I know we will. Together."

She barely heard him. Something outside the window had caught her attention. A ruddy glow that hadn't been there before. Zerie hurried over and peered out. The full moon was red—a deep, blood red. Zerie staggered back, horrified.

A loud cracking sound split the air, and an orange flame leapt up from the floor of her bedchamber.

"Look out!" Ned cried, pulling Zerie away as the flame grew to a blaze, spitting and crackling in shades of red and orange.

"What's going on?" Zerie cried.

"I don't know." Ned's voice was steady, but his hand shook on her arm. He was as frightened as she was.

The flames grew higher, reaching almost to the vaulted stone ceiling of the room. Then a blackness filled the center of the fire, a strange void in the orange light. And in the center of the void, blue as a summer sky and at least a foot wide each, were two gigantic eyes.

.4.

"What is that?" Zerie cried, terrified.

"I don't know, but it's not good." Ned stepped between Zerie and the flames, his flirty behavior vanishing as he snapped into soldier mode. "We should get away from it."

Zerie was already moving toward the door. The huge eyes were so unnatural that she just wanted to be someplace where they couldn't see her.

Tabitha and Vashti were in the hallway when Zerie got there.

"There's a pair of fiery eyes in my room!" Vashti cried before Zerie could say a word. "Right in the middle of the floor."

"In my room, too," Tabitha added quietly, her cheeks pale. "What is it?"

"It's Glinda." Princess Ozma appeared at the end of the hallway. "The eyes can be seen in every room of the palace." She beckoned them closer, but before Zerie reached her, another magical fire sputtered up from the floor, the flames roaring like a hundred lions. The same terrifying eyes opened, blinked twice, and then fixed themselves on Ozma.

"Beware!" A strange, low voice spoke from the flames. "Remember that I possess the Silver Mirror, which sees all places at all times. Wherever you may tread on the Land of Oz, you shall not be hidden from me."

Zerie glanced at her friends. Vashti had wrapped her arms around herself, fear in her eyes. Tabitha took a step closer to Ned, reaching out to hold his hand. Princess Ozma stood, head held high, staring right into the enormous eyes.

"Beware, Ozma! Your days as sovereign are coming to an end," the voice boomed.

The fire leapt higher, flames licking the ceiling, threatening to overtake the princess. Zerie caught her breath, frightened. But Ozma took a step forward, then another, walking right into the blaze without a trace of worry.

The inferno vanished instantly.

Vashti let out her breath in a relieved sigh. "It was only a vision. It wasn't real."

"It was real enough, I'm afraid," Princess Ozma said. "The warning it contained was genuine, even if the fire wasn't."

"What did she mean, a mirror that sees everywhere?" Tabitha asked. "Is she talking about her magic mirror, from the old stories?"

"Glinda is able to make her mirror show her whatever she wishes to see, even though those she watches are not aware of her," Ozma said. "It is a fearsome power."

"So she could be watching us right now?" Vashti whispered, glancing around the hallway.

"If she can see everything we do, how can she ever be defeated?" Tabitha asked.

And how will I ever be able to rescue Brink? Zerie wondered.

Ozma held out her arms as if to embrace them, and the three girls gathered close to her. The princess tipped her head toward theirs and whispered, "The

Mirror is strong, but there are limits to its power. Follow me."

She led the way down the hall, through the emerald door again, and down the gently sloping tunnel, not stopping until they reached the cavern underneath the Forbidden Fountain. There, on the green sand next to the cold, clear water of the underground lake, Ozma turned and looked at them with a sorrowful expression.

"I had thought there would be more time for you girls to rest and grow your strength," she said. "But Glinda's message is clear: She is coming after me. We must move against her right away. Tonight."

Zerie's heart sank at the thought of doing anything else tonight. She hadn't slept for even a few minutes, and it had been two days of fear and stress before that, with very little sleep. Between the confusion about who was good and who was bad, and the worry about Brink, Zerie felt exhausted and overwhelmed. She wasn't sure she had the energy to fight anymore at all.

Vashti tugged at her long, dark braid, something she always did when she was nervous. "Don't you think Glinda is watching us? Or is it too dark down here for her to see us?" The stone of the cave was shot through with veins of bright green, which glowed enough to illuminate the entire cave. Still, it was dim.

"The answer was in her exact words," Ozma replied. "A sorceress is nothing if not exact. 'Wherever you may tread on the Land of Oz, you shall not be hidden from me.' We are not treading on the Land of Oz right now."

Tabitha's eyes narrowed thoughtfully. "We're underneath Oz, you mean. This cavern is underground. So it doesn't count?"

"It is the limit of Glinda's power. She said wherever we tread on Oz, we're in danger. That means if we want to reach her, or work against her, we must be careful not to tread on Oz," Ozma explained.

"So we can attack her from the air," Zerie said, a small ray of hope piercing the dejection she'd been feeling. "Or from underground. Either way, we're not treading on Oz. She can't see us coming."

"I can levitate!" Vashti offered. "I've gotten really good at it."

"That's true—Vashti levitated us over whole trenches during our travels," Zerie agreed. "Our feet never touched the ground."

"It is a valuable talent," Ozma said. "But can you

levitate an entire army? Glinda and the Nome King have an army, which means I must counterattack with all of my military forces."

Vashti bit her lip. "I don't think I'm strong enough to do that."

"Your soldiers can defeat Glinda's, can't they?" Tabitha asked Princess Ozma. She slipped her hand through Ned's arm. "I know how well trained they are," she added, beaming up at him.

Ned stiffened at her touch, glancing back and forth between Tabitha and Zerie. He looked confused.

"I don't know," Princess Ozma admitted. "The soldiers who guard the Emerald City are certainly wonderful, but there hasn't been a war in Oz for many, many years. I hate the thought of fighting."

"We are ready to do whatever it takes to protect the people of Oz," Ned said. "Though none of us have ever battled a rock man before."

Everyone was silent for a moment, and Zerie wondered if they were all as terrified by the stone creatures as she was. She thought of her parents, and her Grammy, and all her brothers and sisters. What would happen to them if the Nome King's servants invaded the village?

"I have a plan, one that I hope will prevent war from coming to the people of Oz," the princess said. "We must attack Glinda at her palace before she can bring her army here to the city. If we can defeat her in her home, the rest of Oz will be safe."

"Will you do it with magic? Are you stronger than Glinda?" Zerie asked.

Princess Ozma sighed. "It's not a question of strength. My magic is different from Glinda's—she is a sorceress, skilled in casting enchantments. I am a fairy. I don't have a magical talent, and I don't cast spells. I simply am a magical creature."

"Well, you have us. We will all help," Vashti declared. Zerie and Tabitha nodded.

"We will attack Glinda on three fronts: from the air, on foot, and from below," Ozma said. "I will advance with my army along the road of yellow brick in order to draw Glinda's attention. If she is busy watching me, she may not notice you girls advancing from above and below."

Vashti shot Zerie a concerned look. "You mean . . . we won't be together?"

"No. To have three fronts, we will need to separate," Ozma replied. "One of you will come with me on foot, one will go by air, and one will be below ground."

Tabitha's pretty face was etched with worry, and Vashti looked pale. "But friends are strongest together," Zerie said. "Our talents are more powerful when we work with one another."

"I know." Ozma laid her small, cool hand on Zerie's arm. "You will have to learn to trust your own strength now. And remember, you are still together— you are all working for the good of Oz."

"That's true," Vashti said in a choked voice.

But it doesn't feel the same, Zerie thought. She knew her friends were thinking that, too. She'd just spent days and days traveling with Brink and Vashti, and that journey had been hard. She didn't want to think about how much harder it would be to do it alone, or with an army of Ozma's soldiers whom she didn't even know.

"Whoever goes by air will travel with the Winged Monkeys aboard an airship," Ozma said, as if she knew what Zerie's worry was. "The Monkeys have their own commander, and you will be there to provide help whenever your magical talent is called for. You will travel by night, so that Glinda will have a harder time seeing you. However, the airships are fast, so you will be the first ones to arrive. You will be the first to attack. Hopefully Glinda and her forces will be tired from that fight, so when we arrive by ground, we have a better chance of winning."

As the princess spoke, Vashti reached out and took Zerie's hand. Zerie felt her shoulders relax—for now, at least, she had her friends.

"Whoever comes with me will ride on horseback, and we will lead the forces of Oz along the road of yellow brick," Ozma went on. "The soldiers are on foot, so it will be slow going. That's all right, since we are mainly going to serve as a decoy, something to distract Glinda from our true plan."

"Do you need one of us with you?" Tabitha asked. "You'll have the soldiers for protection, and our magic is no match for yours."

"Since we will be the ones Glinda is watching, I imagine that she will send small forces to harass us," Ozma replied. "Soldiers or spies or hostile creatures. Those of us on the road will be in the most danger during our journey."

"So having more magic to help will be better," Zerie said.

"Exactly," Ozma said, smiling at her. "The third of you will play the most important role. You will be the one to surprise Glinda from below. She will see us on the road, and she will most likely see the Monkeys in the air. But hopefully she will not see the one below Oz."

"So one of us will be underground for the entire journey to Glinda's Palace?" Vashti asked. "Is that even possible?"

"Are there secret tunnels below the earth?" Zerie asked. "Wouldn't the Nome King know about them? Tunnels and mines are his domain."

"Not tunnels," Ozma said. "Something better." Slipping off her golden shoes and gathering the skirts of her gown in her arms, Ozma ran lightly across the green sand and into the underground lake. She gasped a little as the icy water hit her skin, and her beautiful face lit up in a smile.

Zerie shivered, remembering how cold the Water of Oblivion had been when she'd been forced into the Forbidden Fountain. But the princess didn't seem to mind it. She waded into the lake until the water reached her knees, then stopped. Ozma bent gracefully and scooped up a handful of water. Holding it to her lips, she blew softly on it, then released the water back into the lake.

Immediately, the lake began to move. It spun in an ever-widening circle from where Ozma had dropped it, and when the circle reached the shore, it broke into bubbles as though it were boiling.

"Look at the waves," Tabitha murmured, nodding toward the back of the cave. Far across the lake, high waves had begun to rise and break on the surface.

"That last wave almost reached the ceiling," Vashti pointed out. "What's happening?"

"It's magic," Zerie said. "Ozma's breath woke up the water."

"But why?" Ned asked.

The tallest wave was moving toward them faster and faster. Princess Ozma didn't seem worried. She simply stepped back as it approached, her bare feet reaching the green sand just as the huge wave broke and crashed around her. Foam bubbled and hissed at her toes, and within it, a large fish lay gasping for air.

"It's beautiful," Tabitha whispered.

Zerie and Vashti nodded. The fish looked green at first, but then its iridescent scales seemed to change to shades of blue, then purple, red, orange, and yellow.

Ozma knelt on the sand and laid a hand on the fish. Immediately, it stopped gasping and lay quietly, watching the princess in contentment.

"Did you make it so she's able to breathe?" Zerie asked, surprised.

The princess nodded. "Magic can do a lot when it comes to adapting the creatures of water and air." She stood up and arranged the skirts of her long gown, smoothing them until they were perfect.

"Now," said Princess Ozma, "we find our path."

.5.

Brink lay on the stone floor as the last sliver of light disappeared again. During his second time around the clockwork prison, he hadn't tried to explore his cell. He had thought vaguely about counting, to see if he could figure out how long the interval was between feedings. But he'd barely gotten to five minutes before giving up. Maybe they would feed him twice a day, maybe only once a day. Brink didn't really care. It was the light that mattered to him, not the food.

This time, when he'd seen the crack appear in the wall and the torchlight start to shine into his cell, Brink had run to the opening. He'd been desperate to see all he could of that chamber beyond his dark room. Alone, without light, he had begun to wonder if he'd imagined the world outside. The axle room and the guards proved that he hadn't.

They had yelled at him to move back again, and they'd given him bread and water. Meanwhile, Brink had spent every single second staring at the torches, and at the slowly spinning clockwork gear shaft, and at the stone doorway beyond it, which Brink imagined must have led to stairs and freedom and sunlight.

Would he ever see the sun again?

When the darkness returned, Brink lay down on the floor without eating. The movement of the rock sent vibrations through his body, and the low grumbling of the movement combined with the thick stone walls blocked out any other sound he might've been able to hear.

"Which is worse? The dark? Or being alone?" he said out loud. Back home, he would've been embarrassed by talking to himself, but here he only wished the sound of his voice brought him more comfort.

No matter how dangerous or uncomfortable it had gotten on the road to Glinda's Palace, at least he had been with Zerie and Vashti. Even when they were all fighting, they had been a team. Brink had never had that before. He'd always felt that his brother, Ned, didn't want him around, that he had been keeping secrets from Brink. There were only the two of them, but they'd never been a team.

Of course, now he understood why. Ned actually *had* been keeping secrets. Ned had been a spy for Ozma. Or was it for Glinda?

"I guess it doesn't matter," he said into the still air. Glinda supported Ozma's ban on magic, so a spy for Ozma was a spy for Glinda. "Either way, my brother was always against me. Zerie and Vashti were the only friends I ever had. At least they got to face their punishment together. I have to rot in a dungeon alone."

Someone snorted.

Brink sat bolt upright. His heart pounded hard . . . first in surprise, then in fear. "Is someone there?" he called. He felt ashamed of how much his voice shook. If there was someone, or something, in his cell, he couldn't see it. The darkness had seemed oppressive before, but now it felt ominous. He could be trapped in here with a creature that he couldn't see, with no way to escape and no help.

"Hello?" Brink said.

There was no answer, and no other sound.

Had he imagined that snort? Was he losing his mind?

He climbed slowly to his feet and forced himself to take a few steps forward. When he reached the wall, he did the same long, careful walk around the perimeter of the room that he'd done before. The only difference was that this time he kept thinking he might stumble over something or crash into something. Or be grabbed by something.

Finally, Brink gave up. He hadn't heard another sound since that first one. He hadn't come across anything else in the dark cell besides his cup of water and his crust of bread. He was by himself in the dark, just as he had been all along.

But sitting on the cold stone floor, his back against the comforting solidity of the wall, Brink couldn't shake the feeling that he wasn't alone.

I wish Zerie were here, he thought for the hundredth time. Even in the blackness, where he couldn't see her beautiful green eyes or her luscious red curls, it would be a comfort to simply hold her hand or hear her voice.

Could he do that? Make an illusion of a voice? Trying to do an illusion of light hadn't worked, but maybe a sound would. He'd never tried to make sound before, but there was no reason he couldn't.

Brink thought about Zerie. Zerie on the reddish dirt road outside his house, chatting with Ned about clockwork as Brink looked on from his upstairs window.

"Not that one," Brink muttered. Thinking about Zerie's crush on his traitorous brother would only upset him, and he needed to be calm to use his talent. He took a deep breath and tried again.

Zerie in the forest near home, talking and laughing with Vashti and Tabitha as they practiced their talents. Zerie in Pa Underhill's garden, whispering with him and Vashti and the Glass Cat as they made their plans to ask Glinda for help. Zerie's voice in the darkness as they fled from the Winged Monkeys—Tabitha had made them invisible to protect them, but Brink could hear Zerie's voice, and he'd known she was safe.

"That's the one," he whispered. He focused on that memory. Airships floating above their village, a Winged Monkey with a spear coming after them, and Zerie's voice in the night. Zerie telling him where they would meet on the road of yellow brick—at the first sycamore tree. He thought of the sound of her voice, the musical way she said "sycamore." Zerie's voice was deep for a girl, and there was always a sort of lilting playfulness in it. Even when she was scared, she always sounded cheerful, like a brook trilling over a tiny waterfall.

Zerie's voice.

Zerie's voice.

Zerie's voice.

Brink held his breath, trying to push her voice out of his mind and into the air. Just one word would make the illusion worthwhile. Just one second of hearing her voice.

Nothing happened.

Brink felt tears spring to his eyes. His talent wouldn't work here. He had to accept that. He would never hear Zerie's voice again.

"I'm trapped and no one is looking for me and there's no way to escape," he said bitterly. "I'll never hear *any* friendly voice again."

Another snort came from the darkness. "Look in the mirror," someone said.

.6.

Zerie couldn't tear her eyes away from the iridescent scales of the fish. She'd never seen such a beautiful creature before . . . but she couldn't even guess how it was going to lead them on the path to war with Glinda.

"This fish was a gift from my friend, Prince Inga of the Faraway Isles," Princess Ozma said. "Or, rather, the fish holds a gift from Prince Inga."

"I thought a fish seemed like an odd gift," Vashti murmured.

Zerie nodded. "Especially from a prince."

Princess Ozma smiled. "It was a way of keeping the treasure safe. You see, Inga told me that this gift was only to be used in a time of desperate need, for it is very powerful."

"Our need is certainly desperate," Tabitha said.

"Inside this fish are three pearls, Prince Inga's most prized possessions," Ozma said. "Each pearl holds a different power, and each governs a different element. I don't think it is a coincidence that the three of you have come to me in this hour of need, and that there are three pearls. By choosing a pearl, each of you will find your fate."

Zerie and her best friends nodded. Then there was an awkward silence. Nobody moved. Princess Ozma seemed to be waiting for something.

"How . . . how do we choose the pearls?" Zerie finally asked.

Ozma's eyebrows shot up in surprise. "Why, by reaching into the fish's mouth, of course," she said. "She's quite tame."

"Oh." Tabitha wrinkled her perfect nose.

"But . . . but it's a fish mouth," Vashti said, grimacing. "I know you say there's treasure inside, but . . ."

Zerie didn't like the idea of sticking her hand into a slimy fish, either. But this was their way forward, their path toward defeating Glinda and saving Brink. She glanced over at Ned, who was already looking back at her. He smiled and nodded toward the fish. So Zerie took a deep breath, knelt down on the soft green sand, and reached out to open the fish's mouth.

Its greenish-gold eyes followed her as she gently stuck her hand inside. It wasn't nearly as wet and disgusting as Zerie had been expecting. The fish's mouth felt smooth and soft, and Zerie's fingers found something hard and round almost immediately. Zerie felt a jolt of shock—she hadn't been expecting a pearl so large. She drew it out and held it up for the others to see.

The pearl was the size of a marble and as blue as the noon sky.

"It's beautiful," Vashti breathed.

"It's *blue*," Tabitha put in. "I didn't know pearls could be blue."

"Blue is the color representing its element," Ozma told them. "Blue is for water."

Zerie gazed at the gem in her palm. "Water," she murmured.

"I'll go next," Vashti said. "I want to get it over with." She made a face as she stuck her hand into the fish's mouth, but in only a second she had pulled out a pearl the same size as Zerie's. This one was as green as the city above them.

"Green for earth," Princess Ozma explained.

Tabitha went next, moving quickly and gracefully once she had gathered up the courage to stick her hand inside a fish. Her pearl was golden.

"Gold for air," Ozma said.

Princess Ozma nodded to Ned, and he picked up the fish and gently tossed it into the lake. It vanished with a glint of green.

"The pearls have other powers as well," Ozma told them. "The blue one will keep its owner from harm. The green one will give its owner vast strength. And the gold one will give its owner great wisdom."

Vashti's green pearl floated softly into the air, and Vashti smiled. "I never expected Ozma to give me vast strength," she said to the princess. "We spent years thinking that you didn't want us to use our talents at all, but now I can use mine right in front of you."

Ozma smiled, too, watching Vashti's levitating pearl. "I'm grateful to you—all of you—for being willing to use your talents to help me protect the Land of Oz."

Zerie sighed. For a brief moment, she'd been so

wrapped up in the magic of this underground lake, mesmerized by Ozma and the pearls, that she'd managed to forget the danger they were facing. But Ozma's reminder brought her spirits down again.

"You said the pearls would show us our fate," she said.

"Yes," Ozma replied. "Now we know. Tabitha is air, so she will join the Winged Monkeys in their airships. Vashti is earth, so she will accompany me and ride with my army. Zerie is water, so she will be the one to take a secret journey, the one who will pierce Glinda's defenses from below."

Princess Ozma took Zerie's hand and spoke in a serious tone. "Yours is the most important task, Zerie. Our job is to distract Glinda, to draw her gaze outward, away from her palace. While she is looking out, you will sneak in. Once you are inside her palace, you must find your way to the gates and open them to let us in."

"But this pearl means water. What does water have to do with it?" Zerie asked. "You said one of us would go underground."

"We *are* underground," Ozma pointed out. She raised her slender arms, and the lake began to glow with a soft blue light. Ripples on the surface created tiny pools of ethereal blue radiance, and the green veins in the walls turned a peaceful aqua color. Zerie felt as if the color itself had a noise, a musical hum that echoed off of the stone all around them.

"Singing," Tabitha murmured, enchanted.

Zerie glanced at her in surprise. "You hear it, too?"

"Like a harp, or . . ." Vashti's voice trailed off. She was staring at the water with wide eyes.

Zerie turned to look. The underground lake was filling with people. Young women and men rose from the water, long hair trailing behind them, their mouths open in song. As Zerie watched, one silver-haired girl dove beneath the surface, her muscular body curving through the crystal-clear Water of Oblivion until her long, silvery tail emerged, kicking to propel her toward shore.

"They're mermaids!" Zerie gasped.

Ozma nodded, beaming. "Aren't they beautiful?"

"They are. All of them," Vashti breathed.

"Underneath the Land of Oz are hidden pools and seas and rivers that connect to the Nonestic Ocean far beyond," the princess said. "Most people don't know about them because they are part of a magic that is more ancient than Oz itself. But by following the mer-people and traveling through the waterways, Zerie will reach the river that surrounds Glinda's Palace."

Zerie frowned. She remembered that river. She and Vashti had been walking on a bridge that led across it when the Winged Monkeys had taken them. The river below them had raged angrily, its current moving so fast that it created whitecaps on the water.

Tabitha was worried about something else. "Not all the underground rivers will be like this one, with a cave and a beach and air to breathe. Glinda's Palace is days from here. Even swimming quickly, Zerie won't be able to hold her breath for that long."

"She won't need to," Ozma replied. "Zerie, are you ready to become a mermaid?"

Zerie's mouth fell open. She could see by the expressions on her friends' faces that they were as shocked as she was. "Can you do that?"

"I can. But first you should say goodbye," Ozma told her.

"Oh." Zerie looked at her friends, thrown by the idea of leaving them. Was it really happening right this instant? She didn't feel ready to be on her own yet.

Vashti's dark eyes were wide and brimming with

tears as Zerie hugged her. "I wish we could all go in the same group," Vashti whispered. "You and I have been together through this whole thing."

"I know," Zerie replied. "I'll be thinking of you and Tabitha all the time."

"Me too." Vashti wiped her eyes and smiled bravely.

Tabitha wrapped her arms around Zerie. "Be careful," she said.

"You too." Zerie hugged her back. "You'll be fighting Glinda the longest, since you'll get there first."

"I'll be okay. Ned will be in the airship with me," Tabitha said. "You're the one I'm worried about. You're the only one alone."

Zerie thought about that. "Maybe that's why I have the pearl that will protect me from harm," she suggested.

Tabitha brightened. "That's true."

"I'd better get this over with or I'll never want to go." Zerie turned to Princess Ozma. "I'm ready."

"Then stand in the water," Ozma told her. "Now your life as a mermaid begins."

.7.

Zerie didn't know what she had been expecting, but nothing happened when she stepped into the icy water. She looked at Princess Ozma, confused.

Ozma gave her an encouraging smile. Vashti, Tabitha, and Ned stared at her, open-mouthed.

Zerie frowned. Why were they so surprised? She shivered, the cold water making her feet numb. "I'm freezing. When will the magic start?" she asked.

"Zerie, your legs . . ." Vashti said.

I can't even feel my legs, Zerie thought. The coldness of the water was creeping up her body now. She didn't know how long she could take it. Would the water freeze her to death?

One of the mermaids swam close, her long silver hair floating in a haze around her pale, slender body. She said something, but all Zerie heard was a sound like the musical humming. *That must be how they talk,* she thought.

The coldness had reached her chest. Zerie looked back at Princess Ozma.

"I feel like I'm melting," she said, teeth chattering. "Melting and freezing at the same time."

"You're changing," the mermaid said.

Zerie turned to her, shocked. "I understood you."

"Because you're like me," she replied. Her voice still sounded musical, but the words made sense now. "Look."

Zerie glanced down toward her frozen feet. They were gone. A silvery-turquoise tail floated in the clear water, lazily moving back and forth to keep her afloat. Stunned, she ran her hands along it, to her hips and torso and chest, where it blended seamlessly into seashells. The scales felt cool and soft, and she could see now that the green flecks were individual scales of green, and the silver scales caught and reflected the colors and lights around her.

"Why am I still so cold?" she asked.

The mermaid shrugged.

"Will I get warmer?" Zerie said, turning back to Ozma. "Vashti, remember how the Water of Oblivion was like ice when they forced us into it? It still is."

Vashti's dark eyebrows drew together, and she and Tabitha exchanged confused looks.

"They can't understand you," Ozma said gently. "You're speaking the language of the merpeople now."

"So it sounds like I'm singing? Or humming?" Zerie asked. "But *you* understand me."

"Yes. I speak the languages of all magical creatures," Princess Ozma said. She raised her voice and called over the lake. "Princess Sirena, are you here?"

Zerie felt a stirring in the lake, coming from someplace deep down. Then, with a rush of water, a mermaid burst through the surface, the water around her turning a deep jewel-like shade that Zerie had never seen before. She struggled to think of the name of it, but there was no word that matched the tone of the beautiful color.

Princess Sirena was breathtaking, with large violet eyes, a heart-shaped face, and long, thick silver-blue hair. A crown of water hyacinth and fairy moss twined around her head, and her arms were decorated with bands of coral. She stopped about three feet from Zerie and nodded to Princess Ozma. "Greetings, ruler of Oz," she said in a clear, cold voice.

"And to you, my dear," Ozma replied. "I haven't seen one of the merfolk in many, many years. It's wonderful to meet you again after all this time."

Princess Sirena nodded again, but said nothing.

"I know you are a private race, and you don't generally have dealings with we who live on land," Ozma said, "and I appreciate your making an exception this time."

"If Glinda joins with the Nome King, we are all in danger," Princess Sirena said.

"I agree, and I'm grateful that you are willing to show my friend the secret ways to Glinda's Palace." Ozma smiled at Zerie. "Do you have your pearl?"

"Yes." Zerie unclenched her fist and held out the large blue pearl.

Sirena's pretty face grew troubled. "You cannot travel clutching a pearl the entire time."

"I will make it a bracelet," Ozma said. She plucked a golden hair from her head, then stepped into the lake and reached for Zerie's wrist. The hair wound around the pearl, quickly threading itself into a woven bracelet that held the blue pearl securely in place.

"Thank you," Zerie said.

Ozma nodded. "Zerie, listen closely. My magic will last for only three days. After that, you will return to your human body. But that will be enough time for you to reach Glinda's Palace. Once there, make your way to the back of the fortress. A small, forgotten door was placed there by the Wizard of Oz. Look carefully: Glinda's Palace is made from pink rock, but this door is emerald. It is hidden by trees and green plants. Find it, open it, and make your way inside. You will have to sneak through the palace to the front."

Zerie's heart pounded as she tried to picture doing all this alone. "It should be Tabitha," she blurted. "She can make herself invisible."

"No magical talent will work in Glinda's Palace," Ozma reminded her. "The protective enchantment she has put on it is too strong."

"I . . . I'd forgotten that," Zerie admitted. She had experienced it herself, trying to move Brink and Vashti and herself quickly to Glinda. Her talent had simply drained away as they'd approached the gleaming castle.

"Your talent will be there to help you during your journey. Once you are within Glinda's walls, you will have to rely on your instincts, as would any other person caught in the sorceress's home."

Brink is there. If I can find him, he'll help me, Zerie thought. *I wanted to get to him and save him. This is just another way to do that.*

"The pearls chose you for this task. Or, rather, you chose this task when you chose the blue pearl," Ozma said. "Do not fear! Vashti and I will hope to keep Glinda's attention on us, so that she will not see you inside her fortress. When you open the gates, my army will be there to enter."

"I won't fail you," Zerie promised.

"Time, like so many other concepts of the land, will seem different to you in the water." Ozma reached for Zerie. "Take this timepiece, so you will know how the hours are passing." She looped a golden chain over Zerie's head, and Zerie felt the small, cold clockwork piece come to rest against her skin. Zerie studied it for a moment, surprised to see that it wasn't keeping time like a regular watch. It had a face with tiny images of three suns and three moons.

"It will count down the days," Ozma explained.

"A golden cover will move over the clockface as time passes."

"Ned made that," Tabitha said. "And Ozma set her magic around it. It will work even if you don't wind it." Her voice shook a little. "Good luck, Zerie."

Zerie knew her words wouldn't be understood, so she simply raised a hand in farewell. Already it felt as though there was a wall between her and her friends.

"Be careful," Vashti added.

"Hurry on your way, Zerie," Ozma told her. "May the magic of Oz go with you."

.8.

Look in the mirror, Brink thought for the hundredth time. No matter what he did, the voice hadn't said another word, so Brink had stopped trying to get an answer out of it. Instead, he was thinking about what it could mean. *Look in the mirror.*

Was there a mirror in this cell? Brink had gone around it so many times, trailing his hand along the walls at all different heights. If a mirror hung anywhere, he hadn't found it—the only thing his fingers encountered was cold, hard rock. So how could he look in the mirror if there was no mirror?

And what good would it do, anyway? How would it help him escape this prison?

Still, that voice was the only thing that had broken up the misery of darkness and loneliness, and it gave him something to think about. When the light began to creep into his cell again, he was surprised. It hadn't felt like enough time had passed.

Brink immediately began looking around the room, searching for even a tiny mirror. Maybe a previous prisoner had wedged one into a crack in the rock somewhere. But by the time the opening had widened enough to shed torchlight on the entire cell, it was clear that there was no mirror.

Had the voice meant to find a mirror in the guardroom? Brink had heard about magic mirrors in the old stories. Perhaps there was one here, and it could help him.

He ignored the guards and studied the walls behind them. There was the doorway that led into shadow. There was the metal axle—could that count as a mirror? He gazed at it, searching for any sign of a reflection. Certainly that gear shaft was important. If he could make it stop moving while his cell was at the opening, then he had a chance of escape. Of course, he'd still have to get past all the guards somehow . . .

But the axle was tarnished and covered in oil, and it

didn't even reflect much torchlight. It could hardly be called a mirror.

Brink sighed. There weren't any real mirrors, and he knew it. Plus, the owner of the voice was nowhere to be seen. He had to face the truth—he had imagined the whole thing, or maybe he'd fallen asleep without realizing it and had dreamt the voice. His cell was empty except for the hunk of bread and the cup of water that the guard had just put down.

As the torchlit room disappeared behind the stone wall, Brink dejectedly walked over to the food. He had to get his hand on the water cup now so he would know where it was—otherwise he risked kicking it over as he moved around his cell in the dark.

He sank to the ground with his hand around the cup as the last sliver of the opening vanished and complete blackness returned. Lifting the water to his lips, he stopped.

Water reflects, he thought. *A cup of water is like a mirror. If I looked into this cup, I would see myself.*

But it was as dark as a tomb in his cell. Still, it was the only thing to make sense since that voice spoke. Thirst swelled up in his throat as he thought about the water, but Brink knew what he had to do. He would wait until his cell revolved around to the opening again. As soon as the light entered the room, he would look into this tiny mirror, and then he would know what the voice had meant.

He closed his eyes and eventually slept.

Brink and Zerie were in the red stream that ran along the Foot Hills. They'd been there before, on their way to Glinda's Palace, but this time they knew better than to go walking where the Foot Hills might stomp on them. Instead, they sat on a rock in the middle of the stream and Zerie made the water rush faster and faster past them. Brink leaned over, trailing his hand in the water. He tried to lift some to his lips, but it trickled out between his fingers before he could take a drink.

Just one sip, Brink thought, reaching out again. This time, his fingers hit a wooden cup, and he jerked awake with a start. He had almost spilled his water.

Brink sat up, shaking off the dream of Zerie. His dreams were strange, filled with water. He felt almost as if he was hallucinating rather than dreaming. The thirst had grown so strong. He now felt sure that an entire day passed between feedings. It wouldn't have been as hard to go only twelve hours without water.

"Okay, one sip," he croaked. He would go mad without a drink. He had to be able to focus when the light came, so he could look in his "mirror." He lifted the cup and took the tiniest sip, forcing himself to stop before he guzzled the entire thing.

Shortly after, the light began to show, sliding from right to left as usual. Brink had already placed the cup at the front of his cell, so now he knelt over it, waiting for the torchlight to hit at the right angle to make a reflection. The vibrations made the water tremble a little, so for a moment all he could see was wavy streaks of light reflected in the cup. Then, for one brief instant, he saw his face. Triumph swept over him—he'd done it! He'd found a mirror!

Staring into his own green eyes, Brink waited for an answer. For some important revelation. For the solution that would help him escape. All he saw was himself.

"Move to the back!" a guard bellowed, shoving Brink with the butt of his tall spear. Clearly he'd been yelling all along, but Brink hadn't heard him. He'd been too busy staring at his water. Now his cell was already starting to move past the opening. He was running out of time.

Numb, Brink stumbled to the back of the cell.

"This one's still got water," the guard called. "Just soup for him." A second guard passed a steaming bowl, and the first guard set it roughly next to the water, knocking the cup a bit. Just as the cell moved out of the guard's reach, the cup overturned, spilling water onto the stone.

"No!" Brink cried. "No! I need water!" But the sliver of the guardroom was too narrow. In another moment, the light was gone. He would be without water for a second day.

The thirst overwhelmed him, and he felt tears spring to his eyes. Could he drink those? Frantic, he crawled over to the food, located the cup in the dark, and picked it up to drink the last few drops left inside. Then, without thinking, he leaned over and licked the stone floor, desperate for water.

It wasn't enough. He thought he might lose his mind.

Soup. They'd given him soup today instead of bread. Soup was liquid. He grabbed the bowl and lifted it to his lips, pouring the foul-tasting gruel into his mouth. It burned his throat on the way down, and he coughed.

Exhausted, Brink crumpled to the floor and lay still, bitter anger filling him. "Two days without water, and for what?" he croaked. "To look at myself in a mirror? What else did I expect to see?"

An exasperated snort filled the cell. "Others look into a mirror, you fool!" said the voice.

Brink jerked upright, his heart pounding hard. Slowly, a smile spread across his face.

"I should have known it was you," he said.

.9.

"It's time to go," Princess Sirena told Zerie. "You only have three days." She sank beneath the surface, and all of the other merpeople vanished as well.

Nervous, Zerie glanced at her friends on shore. Was she supposed to dive under? How would she breathe? Her nose and her throat still felt the same as ever—it didn't feel like anything had changed except her legs.

Princess Ozma smiled, but Vashti was biting her lip, and Tabitha had wrapped herself in Ned's arms. Zerie could see that they were as worried as she was.

I have to save Oz, and I have to save Brink, she told herself. Taking a deep breath, she shot a last look at her friends and then dove beneath the water.

Princess Sirena was waiting, her blue hair floating about her beautiful face. "We will begin immediately," she said. "I have chosen three of my people to accompany us."

Zerie stared in surprise. The princess's mouth wasn't moving, but Zerie heard her voice clearly.

"We speak in song above the waters, but below we speak with our minds," said another voice.

Zerie turned, still holding her breath, to see a second mermaid. This one had golden hair, though it was shot through with strands of silver just like Sirena's.

"I am Marinell," she said. Her mouth didn't move either, but the voice in Zerie's head sounded different from the princess's. It was strange, but she could tell who was who even though she wasn't hearing with her ears.

"You're going to have to let that air out of your lungs," said a young merman, swimming over to her with a smile. His hair was entirely silver. Not gray, but pure silver like gleaming metal. He had friendly blue-gray eyes, and he looked ready to laugh. "Your cheeks are blowing up like a puffer fish!"

I'm afraid to let go of the air, Zerie thought, even though she was getting desperate to breathe.

"But you have to," the merman said. "Trust us. You're one of us now, and you are able to breathe the water like we do." He took her hands. "Let it go."

Frightened, Zerie shook her head. The merman squeezed her hands. "You can do it."

She really had no choice. She couldn't hold her breath anymore. Zerie blew out the air, and immediately felt like she had to get above the surface. But the merboy held her hands, keeping her from rising.

"Don't panic," he said calmly. "Take your first breath, and then you'll understand."

It was hard not to panic. But something in his eyes was reassuring. Forcing herself to be brave, Zerie opened her mouth and took a breath.

Water gushed in, and she expected to swallow it, to choke, to drown . . . but nothing happened. Instead, her lungs felt full of air and her fear lessened. She blew a breath out of her nose, and instinctively drew another one in. Again, nothing bad happened. She wasn't drowning. She was breathing.

"There." The merman released her hands.

Zerie smiled at him. "Thank you." She clapped a hand over her mouth, surprised to hear her own voice in her head. Had she even moved her mouth?

"You're welcome," he said. "My name is Tryan. This is Niro." He gestured at another merman. Niro had black hair, also streaked with silver. Everything about these merpeople seemed to involve silver. Each one had a silver trident strapped to their back, and they all had the same silvery tails.

Zerie glanced down at her tail. It was mostly silver, too, though she could still see green and blue scales mingled with the silver.

"Green to match your eyes," Tryan said. "It's beautiful. Not many of us have green. And none of us have hair like yours." He reached out and ran his fingers through Zerie's long red hair, which floated freely in the water.

Zerie's pulse sped up at his touch. *Wow, he is incredibly handsome,* she thought, blushing.

"He *is*, isn't he?" Niro said, laughing.

"We call him Handsome Tryan behind his back," Marinell agreed with a teasing smile.

Embarrassed, Tryan snatched his hand away and swam off a bit.

Zerie gaped at them. "Did I . . . did I say that out loud? I didn't think I . . ." She stopped, confused. When the mermaids spoke, they did it with their minds. Did that mean that all her thoughts were being spoken, too?

"No, not exactly," Princess Sirena said. "Speaking is speaking. But we can read one another's thoughts, as well. We've been responding to your thoughts all along. Didn't you notice?"

"I guess not," Zerie said. She felt humiliated. She would have to be more careful about guarding her thoughts.

"Yes, that would be advisable," Princess Sirena said. "Now we set off. Farewell!"

For the first time, Zerie noticed the other merpeople surrounding them from a distance. She remembered how the lake had seemed to be full of them. They all raised their hands in farewell, and she heard a murmur of voices that sounded like a symphony as they sent wishes for good luck and success.

"I promise we will do what we set out to do," Princess Sirena answered them. "Goodbye."

The other merpeople swam off in unison, like a school of fish. They vanished into the distance, heading north. Zerie squinted after them. The water was crystal clear, but after a few seconds she could no longer see them. "Where did they go?" she asked.

"Toward our home in the Inland Sea, in Gillikin Country," Niro said.

"But our route lies south, to Glinda. Let us go." Princess Sirena turned, and with a flip of her strong tail, she sped away. Marinell and Niro followed. Zerie hesitated.

"Imagine that you're using both of your legs to kick at once," Tryan suggested.

"I'll try," she replied. Closing her eyes, she focused on her tail, picturing it as her two legs attached. She pulled her knees toward her chest, then pushed them backward. Her tail gave a thump, and she almost flipped over.

Tryan laughed. "Never mind that, then. It may be that you have to forget your legs before you can move your tail. It's a part of you now. You simply have to realize that."

"How?" she asked.

"The same way you learned to breathe water. Your mermaid body knows how to do it, but you have to let go of your human body first."

Zerie bit her lip. The other three merpeople were almost out of sight. "They're going so fast. I don't know if I can forget that quickly."

"Don't worry, I know where they're headed. I'll stay with you," Tryan said. "We'll just talk, to take your mind off swimming."

"Okay." Zerie thought for a moment. "Niro said your home is in Gillikin Country. How come I've never heard stories of you?"

"Our home is in the sea, and the sea is in Gillikin Country. But we are not Gillikins, nor are we citizens of Oz," Tryan explained. "We don't consider the undersea realm to be under the rule of any human, and we don't interact with humans often."

"Have you always lived in the Inland Sea?"

"No, our people lived in the great Nonestic Ocean originally. Perhaps there are still merpeople there," Tryan said. "But Princess Sirena's palace and her folk have been in the Inland Sea for centuries now."

"An undersea palace. It sounds lovely," Zerie said.

"It is." Tryan plucked a strange-looking greenish orb from some moss that grew on the stone wall of the cavern. "Here. You can eat this. Try it."

"Are you sure?" Zerie wrinkled her nose.

"It's a sea fruit," he told her. He nibbled at it, then held it out to Zerie.

She took a small bite. "It tastes like . . . like . . ." She couldn't think of anything on earth that tasted similar. "It's delicious."

"You'll learn which of the sea plants are edible, and which to avoid," he told her. "Now, we are heading out of the Emerald City Lake, and your Water of Oblivion here mingles with the regular rivers. The light of the cavern will fade. We'll need a lantern."

Zerie frowned and glanced around. He was right. They were swimming toward a dark tunnel, and the green light from the shore was very dim. She couldn't even see the surface of the lake anymore—they'd obviously gone all the way to the bottom. "We're moving? But I didn't learn how to kick my tail."

Tryan nodded. "You began to swim while we talked. I told you your mermaid body knew how to do it. You simply had to forget yourself."

"So you were distracting me," she said, "by talking about your home."

"Well, you *did* ask about it," he pointed out, grinning. "Here! I've got a lantern." He used his long, slender fingers to snatch a passing fish by its tail. It was a square-shaped fish, and the instant Tryan touched it, its entire body lit up with an eerie greenish glow. The fish looked surprised, Zerie thought, but not alarmed.

"It doesn't hurt them," Tryan assured her.

Clearly he was reading her mind. She would have to learn to guard her thoughts better.

Holding the lanternfish aloft, Tryan led the way into a narrow tunnel in the green rock that made up the underground cavern. It was dark inside, and the walls of the tunnel were so close that Zerie could touch them all as she swam, even the ceiling. Water filled the entire passage—there was nowhere to go to take a breath of air. Even though they'd been underwater for a while now, Zerie had been comforted by knowing that she could get to the surface—and her normal life—if she had to. But here she was trapped. Trying to take her mind off of it, she looked around. Up ahead in the distance, she spotted three more green lights bobbing in the current.

"Is that the others?" she asked.

Tryan nodded.

"How long is this tunnel? It's making me nervous to be in such a tight space," Zerie admitted.

"I'm not sure. I've never come this way before," Tryan said. "But I would follow Princess Sirena anywhere she went. She is our beloved ruler."

Zerie thought about Ozma, whom she'd only

known for a day. Ozma was warm and loving and had trusted Zerie and her friends with the greatest secret in the land. Zerie understood why Ozma was beloved. But Princess Sirena seemed different. Something about the way she spoke sounded cold, and she hadn't even come back to check on Zerie even though they'd been separated for quite a while now.

She felt a wave of disapproval from Tryan, and she glanced at him in surprise. He'd been nice so far, but suddenly she had an image of his handsome face contorted and yelling. Zerie blinked, and it was gone. Tryan was smiling at her.

What was that? she wondered. *Did he read my thoughts about Sirena? Did I read his thoughts—is that what that angry image was?*

"We call it Aquaria," Tryan said in his usual friendly voice. "The ancient waterways beneath Oz."

"Oh," Zerie replied, shaking off the strange image. It was easy to let go of things here in the water, she realized. There was so much to see, from the luminescent fish to the lovely mosses growing on the tunnel walls, to the other fish that swam around them, glinting in the light of the lanternfish. Why bother thinking about something that had just happened when there was so much more happening right now? "I didn't know there was a name. I didn't know there was even water under Oz."

"There is water under everything," Tryan said. "The Nonestic Ocean surrounds the Land of Oz, but it also runs beneath it, in wide caverns, narrow channels, and underground lakes like Ozma's."

"And we're going to follow these waterways to Glinda," Zerie said.

"Yes, but it will not be a journey like it would be on land. We have to follow the water, and water meanders," he said. "A tunnel like this may head east, so east we must go, even though Glinda lies to the south."

"Eventually we'll find another channel that leads in that direction," Marinell added, appearing in front of them with her own lanternfish. "You're swimming like you were born a mermaid, Zerie."

"I almost feel like I was," Zerie said, laughing. "I don't even remember having legs. Or at least my body doesn't remember, if that makes sense."

"It does. We mermaids don't separate body from mind the way humans do," Niro said, swimming back and circling them. "The more you let your mind drift, the more at home you'll feel in the water. With too many worries clouding your brain, you can't follow the currents and enjoy the seagrass tickling your tail."

"We can stop up ahead for a rest. Princess Sirena has found a glade of cattails in a stream just beyond this tunnel," Marinell said. As she spoke, Zerie saw an image in her mind of a thicket in the early morning sun, the tall, spindly cattails waving in the breeze, tall enough to hide the mermaids from anyone on shore. Zerie knew it was coming from Marinell.

So this is how they read minds, she thought. *In images.*

A growing light filled the tunnel as they swam forward, and she could see that it was sunlight. Zerie was surprised to find that she didn't feel relief. When they'd entered this narrow passage, she had been bothered by the close walls, but now it seemed natural to be surrounded by water, and it didn't matter if she could see the surface.

When the dark tunnel ended and they entered the stream, Zerie was thrilled. She could see the surface above her, the trees and sky distorted as if through a lens. But she barely even glanced at that. It was the water that made her happy. This stream had a strong current, already flowing when the water from the tunnel met it. The two channels foamed and bubbled as they came together, and the fizziness sent a million little tingles up Zerie's tail. She laughed, letting herself be pushed to the surface. When she felt the air on her skin and the early morning sunlight on her face, she automatically took a breath . . . and it felt just as natural as breathing underwater.

"Are you happy to be back on land?" the princess asked.

Zerie turned to find her floating amidst the thicket of cattails that she'd seen in Marinell's thoughts. The princess's long hair swirled around the tall, thin, bluish stalks.

"I'm still in the stream," Zerie pointed out, joking.

Princess Sirena smiled.

"It's strange, honestly," Zerie went on after a moment. "I'd gotten used to being beneath the land, it feels . . . wrong, somehow, to be up here swimming in a stream. There could be people swimming here, too. Do you ever see them?"

"We don't usually go to the surface," the princess answered. "However, since we took the only way out of Ozma's lake other than the way we came in, I had to come above to get my bearings."

"And we're well hidden by the plants." Niro pulled

at one of the cattail stalks, broke it in half, and took a bite.

Zerie frowned. The inside of the plant was bright blue, and in fact, everything she could see had a blue tinge, from the rocks along the shoreline to the leaves on the trees that overhung the stream. "It's blue," she said. "The land."

Princess Sirena nodded. "We've come up in Munchkin Country."

The land in Munchkin Country was generally blue, Zerie knew, just as the land in Quadling Country, where she was from, was red. In the north, Gillikin Country, things were purple, and the east, Winkie Country, was yellow. Every child in Oz knew this.

"That's the wrong way. We should be going toward Quadling Country to get to Glinda," Zerie said. For the first time since leaving Ozma, she remembered the timepiece around her neck. She checked it, reminding herself that it was counting down rather than keeping time in the normal way. Only an hour had passed.

"Did it feel longer?" Tryan asked.

Zerie was startled by the question. She kept forgetting that her thoughts weren't private. "It did. Or else it didn't feel like any time had passed at all," she said, confused. "That is, I wasn't thinking about time while we were in that tunnel. Maybe I was too busy learning how to be a mermaid."

"Time isn't the same for us. We don't chart our lives by the sun and the moon, but rather by the ebb and flow of the endless tides," Princess Sirena told her. "You'll find that you simply don't think of things now the way you did when you were a human."

"Nevertheless, I only have three days," Zerie reminded her. "We must turn south."

They all laughed.

"There you go again, thinking like a human," Marinell said. "It isn't as easy as turning south."

Zerie frowned. "Don't you know the way? I thought you were guiding me to Glinda."

"We live far from here and have not traveled the ancient paths of Aquaria in many, many years," Princess Sirena said. "The plants and the fish and most of all the water will tell me which way to go, but you must understand that we are swimming through unknown territory."

"No merpeople have taken the waterways this far south for ages now, not since we left the Nonestic Ocean," Niro added.

"Come," Princess Sirena said. She sank beneath the waves, and the merpeople followed her.

Near the bottom, Princess Sirena closed her eyes and stretched her hands out into the stream, letting the current pass through her fingers. Tryan, Niro, and Marinell all watched her quietly, so Zerie did the same. After a moment, the sand from the streambed began to drift, spinning slowly up through the water, around the princess's tail, and then slowly back down to the bottom, falling in a strange pattern of lines and circles.

Zerie moved closer and felt a thrill of surprise. "It's a map!"

There, formed by the aquamarine sands, was a version of the map of Oz that Zerie had never seen before. It had the typical flowerlike shape that she recognized—with the round Emerald City in the center, and the four countries spreading out around it. But instead of the road of yellow brick and the other familiar landmarks of Oz, this map had a series of what looked like a thousand small lanes formed by thin piles of sand.

"These are rivers, streams, and creeks," the princess explained. "And here, where you see the sand lines are not as high, these are underground waterways."

"What are the circles and ovals and other shapes?" Zerie asked, studying the unusual map.

"Those are caves and underground grottos and pools," Princess Sirena said. "We can follow this map, but we don't know for sure that the waterways will be there still. It's been so long since we've traveled them." She bent over the map, tracing their path with her long, slender fingers. "Here we are. This stream leads to the river, and the river branches some miles after that. The fish tell me their red cousins live in that branch, so I know it leads to Quadling Country."

"Is that where you're from?" Tryan asked Zerie, tugging at her red hair.

"It is," she confirmed. "Though we don't all have red hair. It's just the land and the plants that are red."

He nodded, but didn't let go of her hair. Instead, he twined it around his long fingers, staring at it. Zerie found herself mesmerized by his hair, too, which glinted in the sunlight like the brightly polished clock-work birds that Ned Springer used to make.

I have to guard my thoughts, she reminded herself.

The princess was still studying the map. "We will be approaching Glinda's Palace from the east, while Ozma comes straight down the road of yellow brick from the north. We will have to move through these caverns under the table mountain, here." She pointed. "The caverns lead to this twisted tunnel, which lets out near the Great Waterfall."

"Can we risk going over the waterfall?" Niro asked, a look of worry crossing his face.

"We will have to see if it's possible," the princess replied. "It's the fastest way, since the falls lead to the raging river that surrounds Glinda's Palace."

"So we will stay in the rivers all the way to the table mountain?" Zerie asked.

The merpeople exchanged glances, and Zerie saw a fleeting image of a large creature with fire in its belly.

"No . . . there is a Rak sleeping in the bog near what you call Seebania," the princess said slowly. "We will leave the rivers when we reach Snow Mountain. There are caverns beneath the mountain that will lead us back to the vast underground labyrinth of Aquaria."

"A . . . a Rak? What is that?" Zerie asked.

"An enormous beast that breathes smoke, creating a foul-smelling fog," Niro said. "Although it usually flies, it can also swim—just as fast as we can."

"If it catches us, it will eat us," Marinell said.

"Have you ever seen it?" Zerie cried, alarmed.

"No, but the fishes are telling us about it. Can't you hear their thoughts?" Tryan asked.

"I thought I saw an image of a massive animal with a fiery belly," Zerie said.

"Exactly. You're beginning to share our thoughts and feelings." Tryan smiled.

"So you all communicate this way, by thinking? Even all the fish? What about things like crabs and seahorses?" Zerie asked.

"I hear them, and they hear me," Princess Sirena said. "The underwater realm does not invite fighting such as you have on land. We share everything here."

Zerie nodded, a sense of peace coming over her. "It's lovely."

"Zerie, you must understand something," Tryan said seriously. "There are dangers in the waters, just as there are dangers on land. We must all work together to make sure we survive this journey."

"I do understand. You have all been so generous with me, and now that I can share your thoughts, I feel that we're true friends." Zerie smiled at them. "And friends are strongest together."

.10.

"What are these fish called? The little ones that nibble at our tails?" Zerie asked as they swam along.

"Kittenfish," Tryan told her. "They like to chase anything that moves. They consider themselves very fierce."

Zerie smiled. "Cats are always hunting," she said, thinking of the Glass Cat. These little fish weren't as cold and snooty as the cat, though. They looked like tiny fuzzballs, in all different colors from white to tabby to calico, and their whiskers were longer than their whole bodies. Every time Zerie swished her tail, a pack of them chased it and pounced on it, which made her laugh.

"The river passes through a canyon soon," Princess Sirena said from up ahead. "The water runs deep."

Zerie saw an image of steep walls made of blue rock rising on either side of her, as if someone had made a slice through a thick blue layer cake. It was what the others were thinking of. But looking around, all she saw was the same lazy river they'd been swimming in for hours, with the same low shoreline covered with the same blueberry bushes. "I don't see a canyon. I don't see any hills at all up ahead," she said.

"You're thinking like a land girl," Marinell replied. "The canyon isn't above us. It's below us, beneath the river."

"We will dive deep. The current is stronger at the bottom, so it will move us along faster," Princess Sirena said. "I also hear a rumor of an opening in the stone. We may be able to find a passage south without having to go all the way to the branch in the river." Without another word, she vanished beneath the surface.

Niro and Marinell both dove immediately after her. Zerie hesitated. "How does she hear things like that?" she asked Tryan, who had remained with her. "Do you all hear what the fishes say?"

"It's her own magic. She can communicate with the sea creatures, the plants, even the water itself," Tryan explained. "It's why she is our leader."

"Like Princess Ozma," Zerie guessed. "Their magic is more about who they are than about doing spells."

"Are you ready?" he asked.

Zerie nodded eagerly. Tryan took her hand, and together they dove straight down toward the riverbed. The sand at the bottom was all different hues of blue, from the palest sky blue to the deepest purple blue. Fernlike plants grew in bunches here and there, and schools of fish swam among them. She saw nothing that looked like a cavern.

"Because you're looking down, not forward," Tryan's voice said in her head, responding to her thought. He gently took her chin and lifted her head so that her gaze fell on the tails of Marinell and Niro about fifty feet in front of them. Zerie gasped.

They were swimming down, and the water itself seemed darker below them. The sandy bottom dropped away as she followed, quickly descending into a deep gash in the bedrock below the river. The others had slowed down to wait for Tryan and Zerie.

"It's like one of the Trenches," Zerie said, thinking

of the great canyons that she had traveled through with Brink and Vashti. "This hole might be just as deep as the Trenches, but no one would ever even know it's here, because it's underwater."

"Merpeople would know, and fishes, and any other creature who lives in the river," Niro pointed out.

"Of course," Zerie said, embarrassed. "I meant no one on land would know. I guess you see a lot more than we do."

"Not necessarily," Marinell replied. "You see the land, and we see the water. I never get to see a prairie or a forest. Not unless there's a stream running through it."

"I suppose that's true," Zerie said as they began moving forward again, the strong, cold current pulling them between the high walls of rock. "But you also see what's underground—caves and tunnels and canyons like this one. It's a whole aspect of Oz that most people don't even know about."

"That's because it is not Oz," Niro said. "It is Aquaria."

No one spoke for a few moments as they swam deeper and deeper into the dim crevasse. The merpeople snatched lanternfish to light the way, and Zerie was surprised to see that the lanterns here glowed with a blue light.

"Who was that boy? The one you thought of in the Trenches?" Tryan asked quietly. "Is he your friend?"

"Brink?" Zerie said. "Yes. He and Vashti and I made the journey through the Trenches only a few days ago. We traveled from our village to Glinda's Palace. We thought she would help us, but instead she took Brink prisoner."

"You're worried about him," Tryan said. It wasn't a question.

"Yes," Zerie replied. She couldn't help wondering what else Tryan could read in her mind about Brink. How exactly could she keep private thoughts private?

"There's a Wail," Princess Sirena put in suddenly. "Quickly now!" She gave a great kick of her tail and sped after a large shadow in the dark cavern.

"What?" Zerie cried, as Marinell took off after the princess.

"Kick hard, swim fast, catch up to the Wail," Niro said. He released his lanternfish, and then he was gone.

The big shadow was higher in the water than they were, and it seemed impossibly far away. Zerie didn't understand how they could catch up to it, or why they would want to.

An image of an enormous blue-gray animal with a frowning mouth and big, sad eyes appeared in her mind. It was so huge that it left a path behind it where the water didn't push against the many small fish that followed it, moving quickly without making a strong effort.

"It blocks the water," Zerie said, "so you can swim faster behind it."

"Exactly. We swim in its wake," Tryan replied. That image had come from him, Zerie realized. "Wails are fast, and if we just swim behind them, we'll be able to move much faster than usual, too." He grinned at her. "The trick is catching up to them to begin with. Let's race!"

He took off swimming, so Zerie gave the strongest kick she could, and then another, and another. She didn't get far, and Tryan was speeding away.

"Forget your body," his voice came back to her. "Just think about moving fast, and your body will know what to do, remember?"

Zerie felt stunned. She knew he was talking about how her mermaid body worked better when she didn't think too much. But the words he had used—"moving fast"—shocked her. Moving fast was what she did! It was her magical talent. Somehow, ever since becoming a mermaid, she'd forgotten all about it. For now, she didn't have time to wonder why she'd overlooked such a major part of who she was. She had to move fast.

Closing her eyes, Zerie pictured the Wail—its mournful face and its powerful body, the wake it left behind itself, the various fishes following it, and her among them, swimming easily with no water pushing against her. She opened her eyes.

She was there. The Wail was about eight feet away, its bulk displacing the water so that Zerie felt as light as a butterfly on the wind. She still swam, but it was effortless, and she could see by the passing walls of the cavern that she was moving quickly.

"How did you get here first?" Princess Sirena gasped, coming up behind her. "It's not easy to catch a Wail."

"That's my talent," Zerie said. "I'm fast."

The princess looked impressed. "Next time, perhaps you can take the rest of us with you."

"I should have. I'm sorry," Zerie replied. "I had

forgotten about my talent, and as soon as I remembered it, I just used it. I didn't mean to be selfish."

"Isn't it fun?" Tryan called, swimming up behind
them. "It's as if the Wail is pushing everything out of
the way for us."

Zerie nodded, enjoying the sensation of moving so
quickly. The canyon was deep below them, but they
were still far enough down that she couldn't even
make out the surface of the water above. "I think this
is even deeper than the Trenches on land. I wonder
how long it runs for."

The walls on either side were sheer cliffs of blue
stone, with jagged layers of gray and black shot
through it. The fissure was narrow as well as deep,
probably only thirty feet across. Zerie imagined that
the wide river above must look completely normal
from the shores. Did anyone up there know that there
was a secret canyon below them?

Occasionally Zerie saw a crack in the rock wall, and
sometimes eels stuck their heads out.

"It's dark," Tryan commented. "Do you want to
learn how to use a lanternfish?"

"Yes!" Zerie said eagerly.

A low, mournful sound echoed through the cavern,

shaking Zerie's entire body. Even after the initial noise had died down, she still felt it vibrating outward like ripples on a pond.

"I don't think the Wail likes that idea," Niro said.

"His eyes are sensitive," Princess Sirena said. "Too much light hurts them. It's why he swims so deep."

"He . . . he told you that?" Zerie asked, looking at the massive creature in a new light. He was so big that she'd been thinking of him as being more like one of the Winged Monkeys' airships than as an animal.

"More or less," the princess said. "He told all of us, really. You heard the wail."

"That loud sound? That was him?"

"Who else?" Marinell asked. "Wails are very sad creatures. No one is quite sure why."

"But they're always willing to let you know when they don't like something," Tryan added. "This one doesn't like lights, and he doesn't like the sharks who live up ahead."

"Sharks?" Zerie said.

"Can't you see his thoughts? We can all read the thoughts of the bigger animals. Try," Marinell encouraged her. "You're getting good at reading our thoughts."

Zerie looked at the giant Wail. How was she supposed to read its mind?

"You're not. You're only supposed to let his thoughts mingle with your own," Tryan said.

An image of her own face came into Zerie's mind, quickly shifting to an image of Tryan laughing, and then one of Princess Sirena trailing her hand through the water, and of the Wail's sad eyes. Zerie recognized it as a rush of thoughts from Tryan, and maybe from the other merpeople as well.

"Like everything else in the water, once you relax, it will come naturally," Tryan added.

Zerie tried to relax, just letting herself feel the soft water surrounding her, the ticklish feeling of smaller fish sliding against her as they all swam in the Wail's wake. An image of Princess Ozma's underground lake came to her, along with an image of her blue pearl. Zerie's gaze moved to the pearl, which was still secured around her wrist. She'd almost forgotten it was there.

Then suddenly an image of a shark appeared, baring its teeth. The earsplitting wail of the Wail sounded again, and Zerie saw a tear spill from the Wail's eye, disappearing into the stream.

"He hates even thinking about sharks," she said in surprise.

"You saw his thoughts," Tryan said. "I knew you could!"

"But I feel so sorry for him. He's much bigger than a shark. Why is he afraid?" she asked.

"We would need some more time with the Wail to understand that," Princess Sirena said. "Unfortunately, here we must part ways. The Wail will be turning left at a break in the wall up ahead. We must continue on until the river branches, or we find a passage to the right."

Indeed, the Wail was already turning, its massive body swiveling faster than Zerie would have thought possible.

"The water will hit us like a wall," Tryan said, quickly moving in front of Zerie. "Get ready."

As soon as the Wail's bulk was gone, all the water it had been displacing seemed to rush back toward them at once. Zerie held up her hands to protect herself, but the underwater wave hit her full on, sending her flying tail over head.

Tryan grabbed her hand, stopping her from tumbling into the hard rock of the canyon wall.

"Thank you," she said. He squeezed her hand in reply.

They swam forward, and Zerie felt as though they were moving through the thick apple jam her Grammy made every autumn.

"That's why we look for big animals as often as we can," Tryan told her. "It's much easier to swim behind them." He shot her a smile. "Though you could go faster if you wanted to."

Zerie shrugged. "I use my talent when I need to, but if I use it all the time, I get tired." She glanced around the canyon. "Where are the sharks the Wail was afraid of? Shouldn't we avoid them, too?"

"Perhaps he was only remembering a place where he saw sharks once," Princess Sirena suggested.

"I see a lotus forest," Niro called. "Should we stop for a rest?"

"I'm not tired. It was easy swimming behind the Wail." Zerie checked her golden timepiece.

"You become nervous every time you look at that machine," Marinell observed. "Why not ignore it?"

"I can't lose track of time, and it would be so easy to," Zerie said. "But what if my time ran out and I was in a tunnel underwater? I would drown."

"That boy is also in your thoughts. Brink," Tryan said.

"Yes. Brink and Vashti and Tabitha . . . all my friends. They may be fighting against Glinda even now—or at least Tabitha might," Zerie replied. "She and Ned were traveling by air, and they were supposed to reach Glinda's Palace quickly." She spoke the words, and she knew it was worrisome. What might Tabitha be going through? Was she actually involved in an attack? Was she using her talent to help Ned and the Winged Monkeys? But while the thoughts should have been upsetting, Zerie found herself feeling calm. It was as if Tabitha's situation had no effect on her. She was safe in the water.

"We have more than two days left. We can afford to take a rest," Princess Sirena said. "It's rare to find a lotus forest as big as this one."

"It will be worth it, you'll see," Marinell added. "There is nothing as refreshing as a lotus flower."

The princess was already swimming ahead, staying toward the bottom of the canyon.

"But lotuses grow on the surface," Zerie protested. "At least the flowers do."

"These are not the weak little lotus plants you land

people think of," Niro told her. "These are lotus trees, strong and thick, and they only grow in deep water."

"It's getting dark," Zerie said as they swam down. "Would it be okay to use a lanternfish now? The Wail is gone."

"You won't need one when we get to the forest. But I'll show you how now," Tryan said. He stopped swimming and scanned the area. "The lanternfish we usually use are square, but there are different types throughout Aquaria. There!" He spotted a large oval fish and darted over to it, snatching it by its tail.

The fish burst into blue light, puffing up like a hot air balloon.

"They travel in pods. Find another one," Tryan said.

Zerie saw a few more oval fish bobbing slowly in the current. "I see some."

"You have to surprise them—that's what makes them light up," Tryan explained. "Their back fins are long enough to hold them by, so you grab them there."

Zerie gingerly reached for one of the fish, her fingers grazing its tail. It turned and seemed to glare at her.

Tryan chuckled. "I said surprise it. Move fast."

Move fast. Zerie pictured herself in the middle of the pod of lanternfish, holding onto a tail. And then she was there. The fish in her hand, puffed up and glowing blue, stared at her with wide, astonished eyes.

"That was even faster than I meant," Tryan said.

"How long do they stay lit?" Zerie asked.

"Until they forget about being grabbed. They're not too smart," Marinell said. "They get used to you holding onto them, and then they forget that they were ever swimming on their own, and then they get bored and stop glowing."

Zerie shook her head. It seemed so absurd. "So what do you do then?" she asked.

"You let it go and then grab it again," Niro said. "They're surprised every single time."

Zerie laughed. "And they really don't care?"

"Do you hear their thoughts?" Tryan asked.

Zerie relaxed and tried to see whatever images the lanternfish were giving off. "No."

"That's because they don't have any," Princess Sirena said dryly. "They're not hurt or we would know it. They're simply shocked to be touched, and then shocked to be let go, and so on and so on. They're silly creatures."

She sounded so much like the Glass Cat that Zerie had to smile. The Glass Cat had always thought she was superior to everyone else, and she probably would have been outraged by such a ridiculous fish.

"I've never seen a cat," the princess said. "This one you think about, is she magical? I see a gem in her body."

"Yes, her heart is made of a ruby," Zerie replied. "She was a glass creature brought to life by magic." *And I'm not entirely sure whether she's on our side or Glinda's,* she added silently. It was a thought Zerie couldn't stop, but she tried to shield it from the mer-people. Since she saw their thoughts in images, she figured they must see hers that way, too. So now she tried to picture something else—anything besides the Glass Cat. She came up with her Grammy's smiling face. Zerie focused on the image of Grammy and hoped that would keep them from seeing her thoughts about the Glass Cat.

Princess Sirena looked at her for a long moment, but didn't say anything.

Niro swam in front of the princess, holding aloft a glowing lanternfish. "The forest is directly ahead," he said before taking off.

Princess Sirena followed him, and Marinell swam next to her, also holding a lantern. Zerie and Tryan came last. Zerie was surprised that her lanternfish didn't squirm about or try to get away. It seemed completely at peace.

"There. See?" Tryan said softly a few minutes later. "The lotus forest."

Hundreds of soft cerulean orbs shone in the dim cavern, stretching from the floor below them to the top of the cliffs far above. Zerie's hand flew to her mouth. "It's beautiful."

"Now you know why we want to stop." Tryan let go of his fading lanternfish, so Zerie released hers as well. They wouldn't need lights in this forest—it looked as if it was made of lights. "There is a small lotus forest near Princess Sirena's palace," Tryan went on. "Though the flowers there are purple."

"It's the flowers? That's what's glowing?" Zerie asked.

He nodded. "The leaves give off a soft light of their own, but the lotus flowers are brighter." Princess Sirena was already under the trees, along with Niro. Marinell swam back to Zerie, holding a blue lotus the size of her palm.

"Wear it in your hair," she suggested, tucking it into Zerie's red curls. The gentle light from the flower lit everything around her.

"Thank you." She touched the lotus, feeling a little silly. The mermaids had all put flowers in their hair, as well, but it looked natural on them, just like their otherworldly silvery hair and tails. She imagined that it just made her look odd.

"You're as much a mermaid as any of us," Marinell told her. "Now, pluck another flower and eat it."

"Eat it?"

"Yes. They're lovely and they're delicious." Marinell swam halfway up a tall green stem—more like a tree trunk than a lotus stalk, Zerie saw—and pulled a petal off of a flower. She popped it into her mouth, then laughed at Zerie's expression.

"I've never eaten a flower," Zerie said. She reached for the nearest blue blossom, took a petal, and slowly brought it to her lips. It was so good that she grabbed another petal right away.

The merpeople chuckled. "Not too much! A single lotus flower will keep you full for an entire day," Marinell said. "Come with me! We'll explore the forest for a bit."

She held out her hand, so Zerie took it, happy to know Marinell was beginning to accept her. Hand in hand, they swam among the lotus trees. The bottoms of the trees were lost in shadow on the riverbed, and the tops disappeared out of sight above. The forest was so dense that they were surrounded by trees after only a minute.

"If I didn't know better, I would think this was the whole world," Zerie said. "I can't see anything but lotuses."

Marinell ducked under a floating branch with a flower on the end, and Zerie followed. "It's good that the plants bloom all along their length. Otherwise the light would all be concentrated at the top," she said. "That's how your trees on land are, aren't they?"

"Yes, usually. The leaves and flowers are at the top, and the trunks are more bare," Zerie explained. She thought of the woods near her village, where she, Tabitha, and Vashti used to meet to practice their talents.

"It must be strange to see trees only from the bottom. I like swimming all around them, and up and down as far as I want." Marinell dove toward the riverbed, and for a split second, Zerie saw an image of a large blue clamshell. "And in and out of the branches!" Marinell zoomed back up, twining her body through the leaves and flowers, her silvery tail flicking playfully.

"We don't always see trees from the bottom. I grew up in an orchard, climbing apple trees every day," Zerie said as she chased the mermaid through the lotuses, laughing. "And in the Tilted Forest, my friends and I had to climb through trees growing sideways." She stopped for a moment, thinking of how Vashti had levitated them among the trees in that last trench before Glinda's Palace. The Tilted Forest was the last place that she and Brink had really talked. It was where he'd told her that he liked her.

A stab of worry pierced the dreamy sense of peace she'd had since entering the lotus forest. Brink was alone, and he was a prisoner. Zerie had to get to him. She shouldn't be playing among the flowers.

"Zerie!" Marinell's voice was filled with fear.

"I'm here," Zerie replied, snapping out of her worry. "Where are you? Marinell?" She'd been following the other girl, but now she couldn't see her at all.

"Help! I'm caught." Marinell's thoughts were showing a whirl of blue, rushing water, and lotus flowers blinking in and out.

"Marinell!" Zerie rushed toward the thoughts as if they were a sound she could hear. She felt where they were coming from. "Tryan, Niro—help!"

The mermen were already racing toward her. *They must hear her panic, too,* Zerie thought.

Marinell was below her, deep down among the lotus trees somewhere. Zerie sped down, the force of the water pushing her hair back and knocking the flower from her tresses. How had Marinell gotten so far away? They'd been swimming up here only a moment ago. Next to Zerie, Niro was swimming as fast as he could, and she heard Tryan right behind her.

"There she is!" Zerie shouted, finally spotting Marinell's silver-gold hair among the blue lights. Marinell looked to be fighting with something on the riverbed, pushing at it with her hands as she struggled to get away.

"It's a giant clam," Niro said. "It's got hold of her tail."

"Stay back. It will grab us, too," Tryan warned.

Zerie stopped short, staring in horror at the humongous creature below. It was ten feet wide at least, with an undulating shell and a deep blue mantle. Marinell's tail was caught deep inside the clamshell, and the monster was attempting to close over her whole body, trapping her. It closed over her head, and she shoved it open again. And again.

It's why the lotus flowers looked like they were blinking, Zerie realized. *Marinell had been struggling to get out of the clamshell.*

"She must be exhausted. She can't keep doing this," Zerie cried.

"We'll hold the shell open. You swim out!" Niro commanded.

"I can't. My tail is stuck," Marinell said in a desperate tone.

"I'll free her tail while you hold the clam open," Zerie offered. All three of them looked at her, wide-eyed.

"But you would have to go inside," Tryan objected.

"I know, but it's all right," Zerie told him. "I'll move fast."

The mermen exchanged a worried glance, but Marinell's cry of fear decided them. "I'll count to three and we'll grab the shell," Niro said. "One . . . two . . . three!"

He and Tryan surged forward, grasping the rippled edge of the giant clam and forcing it open. Zerie hovered at the edge. As soon as the shell was open wide, she studied the end of Marinell's tail. One thin silver fin lay trapped beneath a large ugly rock.

"Hurry," Tryan called.

Zerie closed her eyes and pictured herself inside the clam's shell, its blue mantle all around her. She pictured her hands on the rock, shoving it with all her strength. She pictured herself grabbing Marinell's hand and swimming out, pulling the other girl to safety.

"Now swim, quickly!" Niro cried.

Zerie opened her eyes. She floated outside the giant clam with the mermen. Its shell snapped angrily at them. Marinell was next to her, her hand in Zerie's. "It will grab whoever it can get," Tryan said.

Without thinking, Zerie snatched his hand and swam—*fast*. Within a second, they were halfway up the nearest lotus tree. She released their hands and went back for Niro, but he was already swimming. The giant clam grumbled below, but it couldn't move. They were safe.

"Thank you. You saved me," Marinell said when Zerie and Niro returned.

"How did you get stuck?" Niro asked her.

"There was a rock on her fin," Zerie said.

They all stared at her for a moment. "There are no rocks inside a clamshell," Princess Sirena said, appearing through the lotus trees. "Only pearls."

"I thought oysters made pearls," Zerie said, absently running her finger over the pearl on her wrist.

"Clams do, too, but only rarely. What you saw was a pearl in progress," the princess said. "It looks like a rock now, but in a hundred years it will be a tiny, perfect pearl."

Marinell gave a nervous laugh and said, "To think I was almost killed because of something so rare. It must have rolled onto my tail when the clam grabbed me."

An image came into Zerie's mind of Marinell, floating free, opening the giant clamshell from the outside.

"We're deep within the lotus forest now. It will take some time to find our way back out," Princess Sirena said quickly. "We should get started."

"It's true, we've lost a lot of time," Niro agreed.

Marinell swam off with them, giving Zerie a grateful nod as she passed by. Zerie stayed where she was, confused.

"Don't be afraid," Tryan said quietly. "We will

make up the time. Once we're out of the forest, we'll move quickly again."

"I know," Zerie said.

"Let's catch up to the others," Tryan said.

He swam after them, so Zerie did, too. But she couldn't shake the odd image that had just come from Marinell. She'd seen the mermaid pushing the clam open from inside once it had trapped her, but why would Marinell have been opening it from the outside? The clam had just grabbed her while she swam past, hadn't it?

Why would Marinell open the clamshell herself? Had she wanted to look inside of it? Or had she wanted to get caught?

.11.

"It's still not working," Brink said. He had been trying to create an illusion for what felt like hours. Just a simple flame, just for a single second. But he couldn't do it now any more than he could on his first day in the dungeon. "Glinda's enchantment is too strong."

"Then I'm afraid you'll be trapped here for good," the Glass Cat told him, yawning. "I can't do everything, you know. I came up with the plan; the rest is up to you."

"Right. The plan." Brink sighed. "You could have just told me what you meant instead of making me think I had to find a mirror. I wasted all my water because of you."

"I had no time to explain. I was exhausted from searching for you, and I needed to nap." Her tone was unapologetic, and Brink had to smile. Even in the dark, he felt like he could see her disdainful expression.

"So you napped for the entire day while I searched for a mirror?"

"No. I snuck out of your cell and explored the castle," she said.

"How?"

"I'm a cat," she said. "I'm stealthy."

"There's got to be another way out of here," Brink said. "Can you think of anything? You know my talent won't work here. You're the one who told us about the protective enchantment around this palace."

"If I could think of another way, don't you think I would have?" she asked archly. "I was hoping that the enchantment would only work outside the palace. But I suppose the dungeons are where Glinda needs protection the most. She certainly wouldn't want her prisoners having magical powers."

"Well, that's . . . not encouraging," Brink said. It was wonderful to have the cat for company, but she hadn't really been very helpful.

"There is still hope," the Glass Cat told him. "Up

in the tower, I saw Glinda's magic mirror. She is watching Princess Ozma and her army as they march toward us."

"What?" Brink turned toward her voice. "What do you mean?"

"Ozma and her troops are on the road of yellow brick, on their way here," the cat spat. "Didn't I just say that?"

"But why?"

"Generally when one brings an army, it's to attack," the cat replied.

Brink sat still for a moment, trying to figure out what in the world the cat was talking about. He couldn't do it. "Why would Princess Ozma attack Glinda?" he finally asked. "Glinda is obviously on Ozma's side—why else would she have put me in a cell? She thinks Ozma's ban on magic is just and fair."

The cat laughed. "Oh, you humans! You certainly are stupid. I keep forgetting."

"That's enough," Brink snapped. "You deserted us when we arrived at Glinda's Palace, like you always do when there's danger. And then you show up here with no explanation about where you've been or how you got here, and you give me an escape plan that requires me to make an illusion when you know I can't. And now you're calling me stupid!"

"I apologize," said the cat.

Brink was so astonished that he couldn't say a word.

"You have been alone in the dark for days, so of course you don't know the news of the world," she went on. "I will forgive your stupidity this time."

"Thank you," Brink said. "What is the news of the world?"

"I'm not entirely sure," the cat replied with no sense of embarrassment.

Brink groaned. He'd never had such a frustrating conversation.

"Ozma's Winged Monkeys took Zerie and Vashti, that much I saw," the cat went on. "But you were still free, and you had reached this palace. I expected Glinda to let you in so you could ask for help. Naturally, I stayed close enough to follow you."

"I didn't see you," Brink said, thinking back to his run over the bridge to the palace gates.

"If I don't want to be seen, I am not seen."

"Right. Sorry."

"Glinda didn't even let you speak, she simply put a sleeping spell on you and stuck you in a cell," the cat said. "I thought that was odd. So I snuck up to her tower and watched her. She looked in her magic mirror and saw Zerie and Vashti in the Emerald City. They were put into the Forbidden Fountain to have their magic removed."

Brink gasped in horror. So it had happened—his friends had been stripped of their talents in the Water of Oblivion.

"Later, she sent a message to Princess Ozma, declaring that Ozma's time as ruler was over," the cat said. "Zerie and Vashti were there, and that other girl, too."

"Tabitha?" he guessed.

"And your brother," the cat added casually.

"What?" Brink cried. "I don't understand any of this!"

"It is rather surprising," she agreed. "It seems that Glinda the Good has decided to turn on her old friend Princess Ozma. If I had known that, I never would have sent you here for help."

"But what does any of this have to do with Ozma's ban on magic?" Brink asked, utterly confused.

"Oh, I have no idea," the cat said. "However, when Glinda looks in her magic mirror, she sees Vashti with

Princess Ozma, and Tabitha in an airship with your brother."

"So . . . Vashti and Tabitha are helping Ozma, even though she took their talents away? That doesn't make sense." He ran his hand through his hair. "Where is Zerie?"

"She hasn't been in the magic mirror since the first time I looked," the cat said.

Brink sat silently for a moment. He didn't know what to think at all. All he knew was that the great sorceress was going to war with the ruler of Oz, and he was stuck in a dark cell.

"I have to get out of here," he said finally.

"Yes, that's what I've been telling you." The cat sounded exasperated. "Glinda is watching Ozma's army approach."

"So?"

"Must I spell everything out? Glinda is distracted. Her mind is on the approaching battle. When the danger is clearly on the outside of her palace, she will not be focused on the inside of it."

"You mean her protective spell might lapse, or at least get weaker," he said, a wild burst of hope shooting through him. "I have to concentrate to hold an illusion for a long time. If my mind wanders, the illusion fades."

"We can hope that Glinda's magic works the same way," the cat said.

"And when her enchantment weakens, my talent will work." Brink smiled. "And then we can put your plan into action. You're a genius."

"I know," said the cat. "Now leave me alone. I'm sleepy."

.12.

"Shouldn't we be heading south by now?" Zerie asked. Her golden timepiece showed two days left. She wasn't worried yet. That seemed like plenty of time to travel to Glinda's Palace. They just needed to find the branch in the river.

"It's hard to read the waters here," Princess Sirena said, a small frown crossing her heart-shaped face. She spread her slender arms wide, as if to embrace the entire river, and gently moved her fingers in the current. "It's as if something is blocking me."

"Maybe if we move forward for a bit and then try again, it will work," Niro suggested.

The princess nodded, then led the way. As usual,

Zerie found herself swimming beside Tryan. He didn't say anything, nor did she. She didn't feel the need to talk—there was so much to see and feel that talking seemed unnecessary. Whenever one of the merpeople thought about something, Zerie saw an image of it, and she knew that they were able to see most of what she thought, too. That was a type of conversation, she figured.

Tryan touched her arm, nodding toward a boulder on the riverbed. "River stars," he said.

Zerie swam over to look. At least twenty sapphire-colored starfish crowded the rock like flowers on a bush. As with so many things in the water, they gave off a gentle blue glow, the light twinkling on and off like stars in the sky.

"Can I touch them?" she asked.

In response, an image came of Marinell with a river star curled around her wrist like a bracelet. Zerie smiled and reached out to brush her finger over the bumpy leg of a star. It moved, wrapping itself about her finger while its other legs stayed on the rock.

"It would match your pearl," Marinell said. "If you tickle its belly, it will wiggle up to your wrist."

"Oh, I don't want to move it from its friends," Zerie

said. She gently uncurled the star and it attached itself to the boulder again. "They're so pretty."

"They like faster-flowing water. It means the current moves quickly here," Tryan said.

"We must be near the branch—if half the water flows south, the currents are disturbed," Niro put in.

"But Princess Sirena should be able to feel that, shouldn't she?" Zerie asked.

"Usually," the princess replied. "But something is wrong."

"What?" Zerie looked around wildly, but saw nothing amiss.

The other merpeople, though, were tense. They'd gathered into a tight circle around the princess, their backs together, and everyone except Princess Sirena had drawn their trident.

A wave of images came at Zerie—fish vanishing, swimming quickly into cracks in the rocks; crabs digging for cover in the blue sand of the riverbed; the river stars suddenly going dark. Her heart began to pound. She hadn't noticed any of these things happening, but the other merpeople had.

"What does it mean?" she whispered.

"Everything is hiding," Niro said.

"But why?" Zerie scanned the area, but she saw nothing scary.

For a long moment, nothing happened. Then, suddenly, a large, smooth body smacked against Zerie's tail, and a mouth full of terrifyingly sharp teeth snapped at her arm. Zerie screamed.

"Colorca!" Tryan yelled. Just before the teeth closed on Zerie, he shoved his trident into the mouth.

A bellow echoed through the water, and instantly a creature appeared, its sleek gray body writhing in pain, its razor-sharp dorsal fin slicing through the water as it fought to get away from the trident.

"What is that?" Zerie cried, falling back.

"Colorcas. They're like chameleons. They can disguise themselves to look like whatever is around them," Marinell explained quickly.

"It's why the fish all hid." Tryan jerked his trident back, freeing the colorca. It fled. "Zerie, find a weapon."

"But it ran away," she said.

"They travel in packs," Marinell replied.

Zerie didn't have time to answer before she felt another strong body hit hers. She dove, rolling over in the water, to avoid the mouth. She might not be able to see the creature, but at least she knew what it looked like now. Her friends were stabbing at other colorcas with their tridents.

Whenever one of the creatures got hurt, its camouflage would drop and it would become visible. In the chaos, Zerie counted two that had been wounded and guessed that at least three more were still attacking. Now that she knew what to look for, she could sort of see their bodies when they moved, because it looked as if the riverbed itself was moving—the colorcas took on the hues of blue sand that surrounded them.

"Zerie! A rock," Tryan called, jabbing his trident about a foot to her left.

It snapped her out of her panic. He was right, she needed a weapon. Zerie dove to the sand and grabbed the biggest river rock she could find. She felt a body slipping past hers, so she turned and brought the rock down on it.

The colorca's head became visible, its small, mean eyes rolling angrily.

"There are too many of them!" Princess Sirena cried.

"Zerie, use your pearl!" Marinell called. "It's supposed to protect us!"

Shocked, Zerie's hand flew to the blue pearl. She'd forgotten all about its protective power. But how did it work? She had no idea what to do.

"Zerie!" Tryan cried, desperate. He was pushing one camouflaged colorca off with his hand while fighting another with his trident. Niro's tail beat the water, trying to move the creatures away.

Zerie felt helpless. Her friends were fighting, but they couldn't win. These vicious beasts were too strong. It was just like when the Kalidah had attacked her, Vashti, and Brink. They'd been forced to kill it or else it would have killed them. It had been the worst part of their journey to Glinda's Palace, and Zerie still felt awful about it. Killing anything was forbidden in the Land of Oz.

But this isn't Oz, she thought. *This is Aquaria.*

Zerie forced herself to concentrate even though the colorcas were creating mayhem. She hadn't killed the Kalidah on her own—Vashti had levitated it, and then Zerie and Brink had held a sharp branch underneath it. When it fell, it died. Zerie had used her powers to speed up its disintegration so that it turned to dust in a matter of seconds.

Could I use my powers to age these colorcas? she

wondered. If she sped up their aging process, they would die.

One of the colorcas had a wound on its side from Niro's trident. It was still attacking viciously, but it was no longer able to camouflage itself. Zerie stared at it, concentrating on aging it.

"I can't," she muttered, stopping. She couldn't willfully kill an animal, even if it wasn't forbidden here in Aquaria.

"Zerie!" Marinell cried again.

Zerie's attention moved to Niro's thrashing tail. He was moving the water to try to move the colorcas away. *That's it!* she thought.

"Everyone get ready to move fast!" she called to her friends.

Then she swam. She swam in a circle around the merpeople and their attackers. And another circle, and another. Zerie used her powerful tail to propel her forward, and held her arms out to the sides, pulling the water with her. She pictured the water moving faster and faster. She pictured a whirlpool forming in the middle of the river, the water rushing around and around. Faster. Faster.

An image came to her: the colorcas, startled,

dropping their camouflage one after another as they spun around in the vortex. It was Tryan's thought.

Then another image, this one confusing: Tryan, Niro, and Marinell spinning out of control, clinging to their tridents. Colorcas tumbling past them. Blue sand and river stars spiraling up through the water.

That was Princess Sirena's thought.

Zerie stopped swimming, but her whirlpool continued. Her body was dragged along with the swirling current, her long hair whipping around her face, covering her eyes.

"Take my hand," she heard Tryan's voice say. "Zerie!"

She reached out blindly and felt his fingers close around hers.

Niro's and Marinell's thoughts were coming to her wildly, in a jumble of images. They were caught in the maelstrom as well.

"It's slowing down," Princess Sirena said.

"Where are the colorcas?" Niro asked.

"There! They're fleeing!" Marinell cheered.

Zerie pushed her curls out of her eyes and watched as the large beasts swam off into the distance, still uncamouflaged.

"You did it!" Tryan wrapped his arms around her. "You saved us."

"I'm sorry that was so rough," Zerie said. "I wasn't sure what else to do. I didn't want to kill them and I thought maybe if I confused them, they would stop attacking."

"Well, you were right," Niro told her, grinning.

"Thank you, Zerie," Princess Sirena said.

"You don't have to thank me. That's what friends do," Zerie replied.

"But . . . why didn't the pearl work?" Marinell asked. "I thought Ozma said that pearl would keep us from harm."

"Maybe it will only keep Zerie from harm," Niro suggested.

Zerie gazed down at the beautiful blue gem on her wrist. "Maybe it *did* work," she said slowly. She looked around at the group of them. "Nobody is hurt at all. We wounded the colorcas, but none of us has even a scratch."

The merpeople looked surprised, and Tryan laughed. "You're right."

"That certainly isn't the way I would have expected it to protect us," Princess Sirena said. "I wonder if there's another way to activate its magic, maybe something Ozma didn't understand."

"I don't know," Zerie said tiredly. It was hard to remember Ozma right now. "I'm sorry, everyone. I get tired after I use my talent in a big way."

"It's not just you. I'm exhausted, too," Marinell told her. "I feel as if my eyes can't stay open."

"Where are we?" Tryan asked, his voice thick with sleep. "I don't remember these pods."

"Pods?" Zerie shook off her stupor and glanced around. The water was different here. It was *thicker*. Some kind of sticky golden substance filtered down from above. It reminded her of the pollen that blew through the air on spring days in her family's orchard. Were there trees along the shoreline?

She looked up, trying to see the surface of the river. "I can't see the top," she murmured. "It's just . . . red."

"We're not in the river anymore." Princess Sirena sounded sleepy. "That's earth on top of us. This must be an underground pool."

"The whirlpool pushed us here," Zerie guessed. "If that earth is red, does that mean we've crossed into Quadling Country? Then we're closer to Glinda. We can afford to rest."

"Yes, let's rest. We can sleep in the pods," Niro said.

Pods again. Zerie turned herself slowly around to see what they were talking about. Behind her was the strangest sight. Long, thin, interlacing stems wound their way through the water and straight up to the red earth far above them.

Not stems, Zerie thought, studying them in a daze. *Roots.*

Among the roots were gigantic red seedpods, some of them big enough to fit three people inside.

She watched as Niro reached into one pod and scooped out the round, reddish seeds inside, each of them as big as her little brother's favorite toy ball. He sent them floating lazily up toward the roof of this strange cavern. As they passed Zerie, more of the thick golden ooze dripped from them.

"They're plants," she murmured.

Marinell was already asleep, curled inside a pod. Niro helped Princess Sirena into another one, her purple eyes closing.

"Come with me," Tryan told Zerie, pulling her toward an especially large pod.

"These are the roots, and those are the seeds, and there's some kind of strange substance inside . . ."

Zerie's own voice sounded like a lullaby to her, and she realized her eyes were closed.

She forced them open. This wasn't natural. She'd never felt this dazed after using her talent before. "Niro, pull on one of the roots," she said.

He stared at her blankly for a moment before he understood her words. Moving slowly, he took hold of a root and tugged it down. The thick golden strands of pollen parted, disturbed, as the flower at the top of the root fell through the thin covering of red earth.

It was an enormous red flower, its petals soft and sweet-smelling.

"It's a poppy," Zerie murmured.

Niro had already let go of the root. He was asleep, floating among the pods.

"Come with me," Tryan said again, wrapping his arms around Zerie. He pulled her into the big pod, his blue-gray eyes closing.

"I didn't know poppies grew in water," Zerie said. "There's hardly any dirt up there at all—that flower just came right through it."

"Mm-hmm," Tryan said.

"They're not normal poppies," Zerie went on, talking through the comfortable feeling of falling into a dream. "They're some different kind, with roots in the water and seeds full of that golden . . . golden . . ."

"Aren't you tired?" Tryan asked, twining his fingers through hers. "I can't stay awake."

I can't, either, Zerie thought. *Because of the poppies.*

Somewhere in her memory, Tabitha was telling a story. Tabitha loved the old stories of Oz. She had spent half their childhood talking about Princess Ozma, and Glinda the Good, and Dorothy the Explorer . . .

"Dorothy." Zerie's eyes popped open. "Dorothy fell asleep in a field of poppies." She tried to picture their route from the Emerald City—they'd come out of the tunnel in Munchkin Country and followed the river, waiting for it to branch off to the south, and then the colorcas had attacked, and she'd made a whirlpool, and it pushed them off course . . .

Tryan's cheek pressed against hers. Her eyes had closed again, and she wasn't sure if she was awake or dreaming.

"The whirlpool pushed us here, to the poppy field," she said. Or maybe she only thought it. She wasn't sure anymore what was real. "We're underneath the deadly poppies. This is where their magic comes from."

"Shh," Tryan whispered.

His silver hair floated gently about them both as they nestled in the seedpod. Zerie felt it tickling the skin of her arms. She remembered Tabitha's voice, and the stories about Dorothy, but why did it matter? Dreams were stories, too, and Zerie was dreaming that she was a mermaid.

She didn't want to wake up. She never wanted to wake up again.

.13.

The scent was incredible. Heavy and sweet, it was somewhere between the smell of Grammy's apple bread and the smell of the nightdrops that grew in the woods near Zerie's village.

"It's the poppies," Tryan murmured, his hand squeezing hers.

"I didn't smell it before," Zerie replied.

He must like me, she thought dreamily. *He's holding my hand.* Zerie snuggled closer to him in the seedpod, thinking about the day he had told her how he felt. They had been perched in a tree, hiding from the Winged Monkeys, when he admitted that he liked her. It was funny—they'd been in such danger at the time, but they were talking about something as silly as romance.

He moved, turning his face against hers, his lips meeting her cheek. Zerie felt him kiss her and smiled.

The poppies smelled amazing. She could breathe in that aroma forever. But they were underwater. How could there be a smell underwater?

Zerie stirred, bothered by the thought. *There shouldn't be a smell.* Smells were for the air, but she was in the water. She was a mermaid.

Tryan is a merman, she thought.

His lips were still near her cheek. They felt ticklish, like the kittenfish who had chased her tail. But a part of Zerie felt like he shouldn't be kissing her. He wasn't her boyfriend.

Was he?

His hand was still holding hers, his grip strong. She felt so safe with him close by. Nothing would hurt her here. It was such a comfortable, sweet-smelling place, and he was so dependable and brave. For years, she hadn't even noticed him, but then he'd turned out to be such a good friend on their journey together. And she'd realized how cute he was. Why had she ever thought she liked his brother?

Was his brother Tryan? Was he Tryan? She couldn't remember.

It didn't matter, anyway. It was all just a dream. A wonderful, happy dream. The best part was knowing that she didn't have to wake from it. She could keep dreaming forever, safe here in the poppy pod.

Dorothy had fallen asleep in the poppies. Why hadn't she sunk into the wet ground? Had the stories forgotten that part? There was water underneath the poppies. Did the magic come from the water? Or was it the other way around?

"Magic doesn't come from anywhere. It just is," she murmured.

"I know," Tryan said, but he didn't open his eyes. His eyes were incredible, such an unusual shade of blue—almost gray, really.

Zerie struggled to open her eyes, wanting to look at his. But his eyes weren't blue, she suddenly remembered. They were green like hers.

Green like the Emerald City, where Ozma lived. Ozma had given her a gift.

The image of a pearl floated through her mind, large and blue and filled with magic. It was warm, the pearl. It was hot.

Zerie stirred, moving her wrist. The pearl was burning her. It hurt.

Give it to me, then. I'll take the pearl so it stops hurting you.

That was his thought, not hers. He was thinking of the pearl because she was. Why had Ozma given her a pearl that would burn her? Zerie wanted to remember another gift. What had Ozma given her? Was it blue like the pearl? Green like his eyes?

"No. Golden," she said. "Like the poppy pollen."

A golden timepiece. That's what it was. A clockwork piece that counted down instead of just keeping time.

Someone made clockwork. That was important. He made clockworks, and Zerie liked him. She'd had a crush on him for years. Was he the one holding her hand right now?

"No, not him," Zerie said. "His brother. It's not Ned I like, it's Brink."

Brink.

Zerie's eyes snapped open. The pearl was searing her wrist, just like that name seared her memory. Brink. He was being held prisoner by Glinda, and Zerie had to save him. She had no time to waste sleeping. She only had three days! Her hand moved—slowly—to the chain around her neck. She grasped the golden timepiece Ozma had given her and forced her tired eyes down to it.

One day.

Shock and fear shot through her, banishing the last vestige of drowsiness. She only had one day left to get to Glinda's Palace!

Zerie glanced around wildly. All the other merpeople were asleep in their pods, except Niro, who floated, tangled in the poppy roots. Tryan was next to her, his fingers laced through hers. With a rush of embarrassment, she squirmed away from him. Had she let him *kiss* her? She seemed to remember someone's lips on her cheek.

Her movement woke him, and he gave her a lazy smile. "Where are you going?"

He was asleep again before she even answered.

I have to do something, Zerie thought. *I have to get them away from these poppies.*

She tugged on Tryan's hands, pulling him out of the pod. Then she pictured the rock where she'd seen the river stars. That was where the colorcas had attacked them and where she'd made the whirlpool. It had knocked them off course and led them here. So if she could just retrace her steps, she would find that rock again, and it would be safe there.

"It won't work," she said, agitated. She had no idea which direction to go. What was she supposed to do? "Ozma, help me!"

No answer came. Ozma didn't appear. But suddenly Zerie realized that the pearl was still burning her. She glanced down at it, half-expecting it to look red with heat. But it was the same beautiful blue it had always been. She touched it with a finger, gingerly. It felt cool. Had she only imagined that it was hot? Was that part of her dream?

No, she thought. *The pearl burned me to wake me up.* Ozma had said it would protect Zerie from harm. Well, these poppies were harmful. The pearl had awoken her. Could it also lead her to safety?

She stared at it. It was beautiful, but it didn't tell her anything about which way to go. Zerie closed her eyes. "I'm going to move fast," she told the pearl. "You'll have to choose the direction. Take me to safety."

Gripping Tryan's hand tightly, she swam. *Fast.*

After a moment, the anxious feeling in her chest

relaxed. She stopped and opened her eyes. They were deep in the water, and in front of them was a crack in the bedrock of the river. Zerie squinted at it. It was more than a crack—it was an entrance.

"Where are we?" Tryan asked, his voice thick with sleep.

"I'm not sure. But let's go in." Still holding his hand, Zerie squeezed through the crack and found herself in an underwater cave lit by strange moss growing on the walls and ceiling. It gave off a blue glow where Zerie was, a purplish glow on the ceiling, and a red glow on the other side of the cave.

"What happened? Weren't we asleep?" Tryan asked.

"The poppies made us sleep, and we never would have woken up," she told him. "I would have run out of time, turned back into a human, and drowned, and you all would have continued sleeping there forever."

He stared at her for a moment, and Zerie saw an image of him crying. She blinked, shaking it off. He wasn't crying, he just looked confused. "So how did you wake up?"

"I don't know. I dreamed of Ozma and . . ." Zerie didn't want to say what else she'd been dreaming about. "I think maybe the pearl helped me. It does keep me from harm. I asked it to get us away from the poppies and it brought us here."

"What about Princess Sirena?" Tryan asked. "And the others?"

"I'll go back for them," she said. "You wait here, and try to shake off the poppy sleep."

She didn't wait for him to answer, she just pictured being back at the poppy field, and then she was there. The three merpeople were still asleep.

First she took Niro, then Marinell, and last Princess Sirena, swimming fast and using the pearl to guide her. By the time she returned to the cave with the princess, Tryan was wide awake.

"The drowsiness will wear off soon," he told her, nodding toward their friends.

"I hope so. I don't have much time left. We must have spent a day in those poppies." Zerie felt frantic, which surprised her. She had felt so calm for the rest of her time underwater. Running out of time had never felt like much of a threat before.

"It will be fine," Tryan said soothingly.

"Not if I don't get there. Or if I run out of time in a place like this, with no air." Zerie looked around the cave, frowning. "Why did the pearl lead us here?"

"There is a tunnel on the other side," Princess Sirena said weakly. "I see fish going in and out of it."

Zerie swam across the wide cave, her eyes scanning the rock walls. The princess was right. Hidden amidst the red moss was another narrow crack. Maybe it led to a different cave.

"It's red," Tryan commented, coming up behind her. As soon as he appeared, she felt calmer.

"The color of Quadling Country. Do you think these caves go under that land?" Zerie asked hopefully.

"It would explain why your pearl brought us here."

Zerie bit her lip, thinking. "I wonder if this is where we begin our journey through the caves under the table mountain. We'll be underground the whole time."

"Zerie, I need to tell you something," Tryan whispered.

As he spoke, all of Zerie's strange dreaming in the poppy pod came back to her. She'd been sleeping with her hand in Tryan's, letting him kiss her cheek . . . acting completely unlike herself. It was embarrassing. She turned away, trying desperately to hide her thoughts. She didn't want all the merpeople to know what had happened. It was bad enough that Tryan did.

Or did he think it had all been a dream?

"It was a beautiful dream," he said.

Zerie looked down at her wrist, twisting the threads of her bracelet. She couldn't meet his eyes.

"But that's not what I wanted to say," Tryan went on. "You're worried about turning back into a human if you run out of time."

"I'm worried about letting Ozma down, and my friends, and the entire Land of Oz," Zerie said. Although somehow, she didn't *feel* worried, not as much as she should. Not as much as she had a few minutes ago.

"Ozma was wrong about the spell," Tryan said softly. "It lasts for three days, that's true. But at the end of that time, you won't turn back into a human."

Zerie's eyebrows drew together in confusion. "I won't?"

"No, Zerie. The change will become permanent," Tryan told her. "You'll stay a mermaid. Forever."

Zerie was so startled that she looked right at him. "What?"

"Don't you want to?" Tryan tugged playfully on her hair. "You'd be such a beautiful mermaid."

"But . . ." *But what?* Zerie wondered. She couldn't

stay here forever. She had her family, and her friends, and she had to save Oz. And Brink. "I can't."

"We can still go to Glinda's Palace," Tryan said. "But we won't need to rush. You don't have to worry as much."

Zerie didn't know what to say. It was hard to think about the world above when she was down here in the water, especially with Tryan so close, looking at her so sweetly.

"I feel better now," Princess Sirena announced, swimming over to them. "Thank you for taking us out of the poppies."

"I'm sure it was the pearl keeping us safe this time," Zerie said, tearing her gaze away from Tryan. "I think it's what woke me up, and I know it's how we got to this cave."

"That's a very powerful pearl, then," the princess replied, reaching out to touch Zerie's bracelet.

"I'll go first," Niro offered, swimming past them to peer through the crack in the wall. "I can see another cave not far in here." He vanished into the crack. Marinell followed, then Princess Sirena.

Zerie was left alone with Tryan. "I don't know what to think," she told him.

"Think about how it feels to move through the water behind a Wail," he said. "Swimming so fast without any effort. And think about how the sun looks through the top of the water and about how beautiful the river stars are. There's so much in the water to love, Zerie. Just think about it."

He swam through the opening toward the next cave. Zerie looked down, taking in her long, strong silver tail, its scales reflecting the red, purple, and blue moss lights. "I'm a mermaid," she whispered.

Was that what she wanted to be forever?

.14.

"It's working!" Brink cried. "I'm doing it!" There, right in front of him, was a candle, its cheerful little flame the most beautiful thing he'd ever seen.

"I can see it, but I can't see anything else by its glow. In fact, I don't think it's actually giving off any light," the Glass Cat complained. "It's more like a picture of a candle than a real candle."

"Oh, you're never happy," Brink said, rolling his eyes. "I'm thrilled to see something—*anything*—in this black pit."

"Your cell door will reach the opening soon," she told him. "Turn off your candle."

Reluctantly, he stopped the illusion. "How can you tell?"

"I feel the vibrations and I hear the gear shaft turning, and most offensively, I smell those soldiers in the guardroom," the cat said.

Brink felt a wave of fear at the thought of the guards. There were always at least three of them in the chamber. "Do you really think Glinda is so distracted that I'll be able to do it?" he asked. "It's a much bigger illusion than just making a candle."

"It's perfectly clear that her protective enchantment has weakened, or you wouldn't be able to do a thing," the cat said. "Beyond that, I have no more knowledge than you do."

Brink thought for a moment and then asked, "She can't *sense* magic or anything, can she? I won't draw her attention by doing my illusion?"

"Well, if you do draw her attention, that will be the end of that," she replied tartly. "Are you going to do this or not?"

"Yes," he said, gathering his courage.

"Then get ready. Here comes the opening," the cat said.

She was right. The torchlight had begun to show through the growing crack in the wall. Brink's stomach filled with butterflies. If this plan didn't work, he could be in even worse danger than he already was. But there was no time to be nervous. He had to concentrate.

It was easier when I had Zerie to help me, he thought, remembering the time he had created illusions of himself and his friends in order to confuse the Kalidahs. Zerie had sat with him and that had given him strength. Or maybe it was that her presence had calmed him so he was able to concentrate entirely on his talent.

Brink felt calmer now, he realized, just thinking about her.

He smiled. This plan was going to work. He would escape the cell, then he would escape the palace, and then he would find Zerie. And if she *had* lost her talent in the Forbidden Fountain, he would help her figure out how to get it back.

"Move to the back!" the guard shouted, as usual. Glinda might be distracted by Ozma marching to attack her, but the soldiers in her dungeon were behaving the way they always did. Which was exactly what Brink needed.

The light grew brighter as his cell continued its slow journey past the opening.

"Wait until the door is halfway across the opening," the cat said quietly. She readied herself to pounce.

The door reached the halfway point.

"How will I find you . . . after?" Brink whispered.

"You won't," she told him. "Nobody finds me. I find them." And with that, the Glass Cat leapt forward, pushing off with her strong back legs and hurling herself right into the face of the guard who was holding Brink's food. The plate and cup went flying out of his hands.

The guard yelled in surprise, causing two other guards to come running.

The cat gave a loud yowl and raked her sharp glass claws across one of their hands, then used that guard's arm as a jumping-off point to pounce on the third one. With a yell of surprise, he fell backward.

The Glass Cat took off running toward the doorway behind them.

"What was that?" cried one guard.

"Where did it come from?" asked another.

"Stop that cat!" yelled the third. "It's getting away." He sped after her, through the doorway and up the stone stairs on the other side. Two of them started after him to help.

"Wait! Where's the prisoner?" cried the guard with the food. "I don't see him."

The other two turned back. "What do you mean?"

"The cell is empty!"

"Look in the corner!"

"There is no corner!"

"Get out of there before it closes again!"

Brink flattened himself against the wall of the stairway for a moment and listened to the panicked voices yelling below him. It was hard not to laugh at the guards' confusion. But he couldn't stay here. They might eventually figure out that the soldier who had chased the cat wasn't truly one of them. When they thought through what had happened, they might realize that an extra guard had been involved.

He had to be long gone before that happened.

Still holding the illusion of being a soldier, he continued quickly up the stone stairs. The walls around him lightened from red rock to pink marble as he climbed. When he came to a landing, he took a quick look around. He was growing tired from holding the illusion. Glinda's protective enchantment must've still been active to some degree, because his talent felt weaker every second.

There were three doorways leading off of this landing. Brink took the one on the right and found himself in a narrow hallway lit by torches in sconces on the walls. The hall was lined with iron doors, and the doors were locked.

It's still the dungeon, he realized. *Just not the deepest dungeon. These prisoners have regular cells.*

It was quiet here, and the hall was dark. Brink slunk as quickly as possible toward an area deep in shadow. Then he sank to the ground and dropped his illusion.

"Very good," the Glass Cat said from the darkness. "See? When Glinda's soldiers look into a mirror, they only see themselves. I told you it would work."

Brink smiled tiredly. "Then you should have said 'use your talent to disguise yourself as a guard' instead of saying 'look in the mirror.'"

The cat stepped softly out from the shadows, sat down, and daintily licked her paw. "It's not my fault you can't think for yourself."

She was so rude. She had been ever since he'd first met her. Brink felt like kissing her anyway.

"Thank you," he told her. "I couldn't have escaped without you."

"You haven't escaped yet," she said. "Now if you're

done resting, follow me. And for goodness' sake, don't make so much noise."

"I'm not making noise," he protested.

One of the cell doors suddenly rattled violently. "Brink?" a voice cried. "Brink Springer, I hear your voice! Brink, is that you?"

"I told you you were loud," the cat sniffed.

Brink ran to the door and looked through the small, barred window.

His brother, Ned, stared back at him.

.15.

"I think my favorite thing is the quiet," Zerie told Marinell as they swam. "Or, well, I suppose it's not really *quiet*. It's a different kind of noise than what I'm used to."

"I hear the rushing of the waters and the seaweed waving in the currents," Marinell replied, moving her body gracefully between the large boulders that filled the cave. "And Princess Sirena hears much more than that."

"She hears all the creatures of the deep," Niro said. "Every clown fish, every lobster, and every Wail. Princess Sirena reads the water the way the rest of us read thoughts."

Zerie frowned. "I wonder why she didn't know the colorcas were coming, then."

"I did," the princess said from behind her. "At least, I knew there was a disturbance. Colorcas are very good at hiding, and they disguise their thoughts, as well as their bodies."

"Of course," Zerie said. "That makes sense."

"What do you hear, Zerie?" Tryan asked. He held out his hand to help pull her through a narrow spot between rocks. This was the third cave they'd found, and it was the smallest. Enormous boulders filled most of the space, and sometimes it was hard to get past them at all.

"I hear the currents rushing, like Marinell said," Zerie replied. "And creatures moving about, and rocks and sand shifting. There's something about it, though, that seems muted. I can hear sounds from a long way off, but it's as if they're coming through a layer of cotton."

He chuckled. "I don't know what cotton is, I'm afraid."

"It's a fabric. And a plant," she told him, then shrugged. "It's not really anything you need down here, I guess. None of you have clothes."

"We don't need them," he replied. "We don't need any adornment beyond what the water gives us—sea stars, coral, flowers, shells . . . these all make beautiful jewelry."

As he spoke, an image of Zerie's bracelet came into her mind, its golden strands woven around the blue pearl. He was thinking of her version of jewelry. *It must seem strange to him,* she realized. His version of jewelry was completely different.

"My family lives off the land the way you live off the water," Zerie explained. "I grew up on an apple orchard. Our apple trees give us most of what we need—food, wood for our houses, shade in the summertime."

Marinell glanced over her shoulder. "Does your orchard have the variety we have in the water?" she asked, raising her arms and gesturing to the cavern around them. It was crowded with large rocks that made their journey slower, but it was interesting to look at. The boulders were all sculpted into different shapes—some curved, some triangular, some thin on the bottom and wide on the top, and some exactly the opposite. Sometimes Zerie caught one out of the corner of her eye and thought it was a person, or a merperson, or a Wail. "This cave is nothing like the one we last traveled."

It was true. The second cave had been utterly empty except for the reddish sand on the floor and the tiny red fish darting throughout, their scales glinting in the glow from the pink sea stars high up on the ceiling.

"Our orchard doesn't have that kind of variety, no," Zerie replied. "But the Land of Oz does. On my last journey to Glinda's Palace, I passed through a desert and a glacier and a jungle."

Marinell didn't answer. Zerie saw an image of her pretty face with a frown, but when she looked at the other mermaid, Marinell smiled.

"Didn't you say we would come to a twisting tunnel next?" Niro asked from up ahead.

"Yes," Princess Sirena answered. "A twisting tunnel that leads to the Great Waterfall."

"I can't find it," Niro said.

Zerie saw an image of the princess's violet eyes, her brows drawn together in confusion. Marinell's frowning face again. Tryan's soft lips drawn down in a frown. As usual, none of their faces matched the images in her head.

Those are their feelings, she realized. *Nobody's face shows every emotion they have right at the instant they have it.*

She'd always considered the merpeople's mind reading to be about thoughts. When she'd received images from them, she'd assumed they were thinking those exact images. But of course that didn't make any sense—they weren't intentionally sending her pictures, they were just thinking and feeling the same way she was. The images she saw were unbidden, thoughts and emotions all jumbled together. Zerie laughed, surprised at how silly she'd been.

"What's funny?" Tryan asked, swimming close.

"You don't know, because you can't really read my mind," she told him. "Can you?"

His blue-gray eyes widened. "Of course I can."

"I didn't mean it that way," she said quickly. "What I meant was that I didn't understand your communication until now. I assumed you were purposely sending thoughts to one another, sort of like talking, only with thoughts."

"Well, no," he said slowly. "When we want to talk, we talk."

"Right! But you talk into one another's minds, so

I thought it was all the same thing," Zerie said. "I'm not explaining this well. What I mean is, when I see images from you, it doesn't mean that you're trying to make me see that image. It just means that you are feeling a certain way, and I see your feeling as an image."

Tryan nodded. "I suppose that's how it works. The truth is, I've never given it much thought. It's simply how we communicate—we hear one another's thoughts, we feel one another's feelings, and we talk when we want to. We can close ourselves off and be on our own, but whenever we want to, we can join in the whole group. We are all together, in every way."

"Do you feel my feelings?" she asked. All this time, she'd been telling herself she had to guard her thoughts, but it hadn't occurred to her to guard her feelings.

"I do," Tryan admitted. "But I know some of your feelings embarrass you, so I haven't mentioned it."

Zerie bit her lip, wishing now that she hadn't asked. They had never spoken about their time together in the poppy pod, and she was definitely embarrassed by it. But if he could feel her emotions, he would feel not just the humiliation, but also the attraction she felt to him, the warmth and safety she'd experienced being with him there.

"Tryan! Come help me search for a tunnel entrance," Niro called. An image of Princess Sirena's frowning face came to Zerie, and she instantly understood that it was a picture of Niro's emotion. He was afraid the princess would be unhappy if he didn't find the tunnel.

"Don't be embarrassed about your feelings," Marinell said, laying her hand on Zerie's arm. "We share emotions all the time, so we don't find them uncomfortable. No one would judge you for being fond of Tryan."

Zerie winced. "You can tell that?"

Marinell nodded, and Zerie saw an image of Marinell in the arms of a merman with the same golden-silver hair that she had. Zerie understood: Marinell was in love with that merman. Now that she realized what the images were, she found it much easier to understand what they meant.

"I do think Tryan is wonderful," Zerie admitted. "But there's someone else—"

An image of the blue pearl shot into Zerie's mind, and she stopped talking, surprised. Almost immediately, that image melted into a picture of Tryan's handsome face.

"Someone else?" Marinell asked, as if nothing had happened.

Zerie blinked, confused. Had those feelings just come from Marinell? Or from one of the others? "Um, yes," she replied. "Brink. He's at Glinda's Palace. It's part of why I'm so desperate to get there."

An image of the clockwork timepiece came to her and then an image of the pearl again. Then, stronger than both, an image of a beautiful chamber made of coral, with a rainbow of fish streaming through the water above it.

Marinell smiled. "Do not fear. We have all the time in the world to reach Glinda's Palace."

"Not if I want to go back to being a human," Zerie replied. She checked her timepiece. "I only have twenty hours left."

"You've already been a human," Marinell said. "It wouldn't be a terrible thing to remain a mermaid, would it? I know you find it peaceful in the water. You like the quiet, and you're beginning to really communicate the way we do. I think you would love our home, Princess Sirena's palace."

Another image of the coral chamber came to Zerie, and she understood that it was Marinell's home, and that Marinell was longing to be there.

"I do love it in the water," Zerie said. "But . . ."

But what? She wasn't even sure. Why would it be so bad to stay down here with her friends? With Tryan? She could go back through the waterways of Aquaria to their coral palace, eating the delicious sea fruits and lotus flowers, playing with the adorable kittenfish. Another image of the coral chamber drifted through Zerie's mind, thrilling her with its beauty. And Tryan would be with her. A picture of his smile filled her thoughts, his beautiful eyes, his silvery hair. Why would she ever want to go back to being a human?

I have to save Oz, she thought lazily. *And Brink.*

But it was like she had said earlier about the sounds—her thoughts seemed to come from a distance, too, as if there were a layer of cotton between her and them.

I don't have to choose, she decided. *I can still go and open the doors of Glinda's Palace, and then come back to live in the water. There's no need to worry.*

An image of the golden timepiece appeared, stabbing through the gauzy layers of happy images in her mind. At the same time, Zerie felt a sensation of warmth on her wrist, as though the blue pearl was burning her.

"Ouch!" she said, shaking her hand to dispel the feeling.

"What was that?" Marinell asked. The pearl shot through Zerie's mind again, and she felt disoriented. She was the one feeling alarmed because of the pearl, but that image had seemed to come from the other mermaid.

"I don't know," she replied. "I'm worried about getting to Glinda, I suppose."

"Well, we're going to have to find another way to do that," Niro said. "Because there is no tunnel entrance here."

Zerie swam over a short, rounded boulder and through two tall rocks twisted like the tornado that Dorothy the Explorer had ridden. On the other side was a smooth wall of rock that stretched as far as she could see to both sides and rose to the level of the roof.

"It should be here," Princess Sirena said, her voice calm and collected. But an image of her heart-shaped face with flashing eyes and a snarl on her normally serene lips filled Zerie's mind. The princess was furious.

As she had done at the start of their journey, Princess Sirena spread her arms wide, splaying her fingers and letting her body float limply. Again, the sand that made up the floor drifted together, spinning slowly up through the water around the princess's tail and then twisting back down to the bottom, falling neatly into place in a map. This map was red, since the sand under Quadling Country was red, but otherwise it was identical to the first one.

"We started here." Niro pointed to the Emerald City. "The first tunnel let us out into the river here." He moved his long finger to a thin line in the sand. "We followed it to the branch in the river—"

"No, we didn't. We got knocked off course and trapped in the poppies," Tryan said.

An image of the poppy pod Zerie and Tryan had slept in popped into Zerie's mind, and she knew Tryan was remembering how wonderful it had felt to be snuggled together there. Zerie felt a rush of embarrassment, and she wondered what kind of image the feeling of embarrassment showed to the other mermaids.

"That's right. It was Zerie's pearl that brought us to these caves," Niro said. An image of the pearl came to Zerie. "Do you think maybe it brought us to the wrong pathway?"

"Perhaps these caves aren't the labyrinth we were supposed to find," Marinell said.

Zerie stroked the bracelet with her fingers. "I feel sure it brought us the right way. It's supposed to protect us from harm."

"That doesn't mean it will find our route for us," Niro pointed out.

"These are the correct caverns," Princess Sirena said, studying the map. "The first cave was that mossy one, and the second was large and empty, and this one is filled with statues." She gestured toward the strangely shaped boulders. "But there should be an entrance to a twisted tunnel. Perhaps it's under the cave floor? Or high up, near the ceiling?"

"I don't think so," Zerie said, her heart sinking. "Look at the stone of this wall. It's completely different from everything else in the cave. It's smooth, and all the other rock is twisted and grooved—even the walls."

"You're right. And it's gray," Tryan said. "That's

been bothering me, but I couldn't quite figure out why. The rest of the cavern is carved from reddish rock, but this wall is plain and gray."

The image of a bent and misshaped man filled Zerie's mind. His orange eyes peered angrily out of a lined and weathered face, and his expression was so filled with rage that Zerie felt the urge to flee.

It was coming from Princess Sirena. "What . . . what was that?" she asked, although she understood the emotion—fear.

"The Nome King," the princess said. "This wall, it's the work of the Nome King. His underground servants can work wonders with rock and mineral, sand and jewel. He's put it here to block our passage."

"But then how will we get to Glinda's Palace?" Zerie cried.

"If he has his way," the princess said, "we won't."

.16.

"Don't touch the jellyfish!" Tryan warned Zerie, catching her hand just before she made contact with the dark pink balloon-like creature floating gently past.

"Will it sting me? It just looks so soft that I want to feel it," she said.

"No, they don't sting. But they're sticky. If you get the jelly on you, it won't come off for days," Marinell said.

"At home, we wash jelly off with water," Zerie said.

"This is water jelly. It attaches itself to you and stays there. And it makes you itchy." Tryan gave her a smile, but the images coming from him were all negative.

Zerie knew he was worried. They all were.

Since coming across the Nome King's wall, they had made their way back through the statue cavern and then found another small cave leading away from the empty cavern. It was so small that it had been nearly impossible to see on Princess Sirena's sand map, but they were hoping it would connect with the twisty tunnel somewhere past where the Nome King had blocked them.

They still planned to find their way to Glinda's Palace, but the fact that the Nome King's power had such a far reach had unnerved the merpeople. Zerie kept getting images from them of that terrifying, twisted man, and she knew that the mermaids were afraid of him.

But Zerie's worry was different. The golden time-piece read ten hours left. Ten hours until she would become a mermaid for good. The thought frightened her and excited her in equal measures. Every time she began to ponder it, though, she forced herself to stop. Her own life wasn't the issue right now. Princess Ozma was expecting Zerie to be at Glinda's Palace in ten hours. If she wasn't there to let in Ozma's army, the entire plan would fail.

"This cave is so narrow," she said. "It's almost like a tunnel itself."

"Except it doesn't lead anywhere. We've reached the end," Niro said. He whipped around, his tail slicing the water like a knife. "We'll have to go back to the empty cave and see if there's another way out."

Zerie's head filled with images of their frustration. Princess Sirena was angry.

"Do you . . . do you mind if I use my talent to move us quickly?" Zerie asked hesitantly. She didn't want to imply that they were too slow. "We're running out of time."

"Time isn't the problem. The Nome King is," the princess snapped.

Zerie bit her lip. "I can move fast on my own, then," she offered. "I've looked at the map with you. I know that after the twisted tunnel, we will reach the Great Waterfall, and that will drop into the grotto beneath Glinda's river. As long as I can find a different route to the twisted tunnel, I will know exactly where to go."

They all stared at her, and the image of the blue pearl filled her mind.

"Nonsense. We promised to take you to Glinda's Palace, and that's what we'll do," Princess Sirena said.

"We would never let you go all alone," Tryan said, smiling at her. "Friends are strongest together, like you said."

"Oh. All right. I just thought you were getting frustrated," Zerie admitted.

The pearl still stayed in her mind, images coming from them all.

"We're afraid," Marinell replied. "Not frustrated. Who knows what else the Nome King has done down here?"

"We didn't know that he had invaded Aquaria," the princess said. "Though perhaps he only dared to do so since none of our people have been to this region in so long."

The image of the pearl faded, and the usual stream of calm, pretty scenes returned.

Zerie relaxed—the merpeople clearly felt a little better now. She hadn't really wanted to go on her own, and they obviously felt safer when they were around the pearl, since they depended on its magic to protect them all.

"So . . . shall I move us quickly? Only back to the empty cavern," Zerie said. "We'll have to look for another exit from there."

"Yes." The images coming from Princess Sirena were as serene as her voice. "How will you do it?"

Zerie thought. "Everyone join hands to make a sort of chain," she suggested. "I'll hold on to the person in front, and I can pull you all behind me."

"Sounds like fun," Tryan said. They all joined hands, putting the princess in the middle. Zerie pictured the route back to the large, empty cavern with its sea star-studded ceiling. She swam.

They were back in the cavern within a minute. The merpeople seemed a bit startled, and Zerie realized that she must have gone even faster than usual.

"Sorry," she mumbled.

"That's quite a strong talent," the princess said.

"I keep telling her she'll be an amazing mermaid," Tryan put in. "None of us have magical talents like that!"

"With Zerie's magic, she could speed us back home to Princess Sirena's palace in no time," Marinell said. Zerie saw an image of Marinell's boyfriend again, and then the lovely coral palace.

And then the blue pearl.

From Tryan came an image of Zerie herself, looking impossibly beautiful, the specks of green in her tail glinting like emeralds, her red hair floating perfectly on the current, her pearl bracelet glowing a soft blue.

Most of their feelings are so nice, Zerie thought. *But why does the pearl keep showing up?*

Marinell missed home, and she was scared. And Tryan was as attracted to Zerie as she was to him. And he was scared, too, she supposed. But still, it seemed a bit odd that they were depending so much on the pearl to keep them safe. They had never really seen it work. The only one it had helped so far was Zerie.

Zerie gasped. The pearl had helped her! She'd used it to find her way out of the poppy pods. Why couldn't she use it that way now?

"Let me see if the pearl can help us find a different route," she suggested, swimming over to where Princess Sirena and Niro were searching the cavern walls for a crack, a tunnel, a door, or an opening of any kind.

"How?" Princess Sirena asked, gazing at the pearl.

"Well, in the roots of the poppy field, I asked it to take me to safety," Zerie said, thinking back. "We're not exactly unsafe here, though. Maybe I'm wrong. Maybe it won't work, since it doesn't have to protect me right now."

"Unless you think of becoming a mermaid as a danger," the princess said gently. "I hope you don't. But if the pearl thought you were in danger of being trapped here, maybe it would magically help you get out?"

Zerie nodded. "It's worth a try."

She thought about what would happen if the golden timepiece counted down to zero while she was still stuck in a cave like this one, which was entirely filled with water. She wouldn't be able to breathe, Ozma wouldn't be there to reverse the spell, and she would become a mermaid. Would it be different? Would she suddenly be as good at reading thoughts and emotions as the other merpeople? Would she forget all about her life as a human? What about her family? Her friends? Brink?

It was so beautiful in the water. Zerie loved the feel of water sliding past her body, loved the ease with which she could propel herself with her muscular tail, loved the way her hair surrounded her, floating free. She loved the colors, the way everything seemed to have a hundred different shades in it. She loved the creatures—kittenfish and stars and jellyfish. Everything except the colorcas.

But it's not my home, she thought. Right now her

senses were filled with mermaid things, but she knew that somewhere up above, Tabitha was in an airship with Ned, attacking Glinda's Palace. Vashti was with Ozma on the road of yellow brick, traveling with an army. And Brink . . . well, Brink was a prisoner. Those were the people she was supposed to care about. And if she stayed down here, she would lose them.

"Help me find a way to Glinda's Palace," she whispered, caressing the blue pearl with her finger. "Time is going to run out and the enchantment will become permanent. Help me!"

She held out her hand to Tryan, and he took it, entwining their fingers. Zerie swam fast.

"Stop!" Tryan cried.

She stopped. They were in a long, low cave filled with sharp red rocks. The ceiling was so close to Zerie's head that she had to curve her body so she didn't bump herself on it. "Do you think this is a cave that will lead to the twisted tunnel?" she asked.

"I don't know why we would have come here otherwise," Tryan said. "But you were moving too fast for me to see how we got to this place. How will we find the others?"

"You stay here. I'll go back for them, just like last

time," she said. "See if you can find a way into the tunnel."

Without waiting to hear his answer, she sped back to Princess Sirena and the others. As soon as she saw them, her mind filled with images of the pearl.

"Yes, the pearl helped," she told them. "At least, I'm assuming it did. It led us to a cave we haven't seen yet."

Princess Sirena linked hands with the other two, and Marinell grabbed Zerie's hand. "Let's go."

Zerie swam again, so fast that the water felt like it was flying by. She tried to watch where she was going, but all she saw was a blur of narrow caves and fissures in the reddish rock. All she could do was trust that the pearl's magic was leading her to the way out. To safety.

Tryan turned in surprise when they arrived in the low cave. "You've only been gone a few seconds."

"So you didn't find a way to the tunnel," Zerie guessed.

He hesitated. "I actually thought I saw an opening, but these rocks are growing over it."

Niro examined the sharp red rocks that covered the floor and walls. "These aren't rocks," he said. "These are crystals. Rubies."

Princess Sirena touched one of the sparkling stones. "It's got sharp edges."

"I guess it makes sense that there would be rubies under Quadling Country. Everything else is red, why not the gems?"

"Maybe this is why the Nome King's servants were in this area. He loves gemstones more than anything in the world," Princess Sirena said. "He could have been looking for this cave. That new wall he put over the twisted tunnel might have nothing to do with our mission or with Glinda. It could just be the Nome King protecting his newest ruby mine."

"I don't think so," Marinell replied. "These rubies are growing."

"That's what I thought!" Tryan said. "I could swear I saw them move. Look!"

They all swam over to what appeared to be a crack in the stone floor of the cave. There was definitely something on the other side—another cave, probably—because Zerie could see a blue light coming through the crack. But the crack itself was getting smaller. She leaned closer to the jagged red stones, studying them closely.

In tiny, nearly imperceptible motions, the

crystals were expanding, creating new sharp—and beautiful—edges.

"They're growing over the opening," Tryan said.

"Not only over the opening. Everywhere." Marinell waved her slender arms around the cave.

"It's the Nome King. He's trying to block our path again," Niro said grimly. "If he fills this room with rubies, we'll be stuck." It wasn't an image of the rubies that came from him, though. It was an image of the blue pearl.

"Go through the crack before it's completely covered," Zerie ordered them.

She slipped one arm around Marinell's waist and the other around the princess's, and pushed them—*fast*—through the ever-shrinking opening. Niro was already halfway through.

"You go first," Tryan told her.

"We go together," she replied, grabbing his hand. They made it through the opening just as the last rubies grew over it, creating a wall of red that completely hid the passage. Zerie crossed her arms and watched, frustrated. "Can he *see* us? I thought Glinda's magic mirror didn't work below Oz."

"I don't think he's watching. I think he's just filling

all the caves in this labyrinth," Marinell replied. "These sapphire crystals are growing, too."

"What?" Zerie looked around this new cave for the first time. This one was covered in blue stones, the most beautiful stones she'd ever seen. Marinell had caught a lanternfish, and its red glow turned the sapphires purple . . . and also showed how quickly they were filling the space.

"At least this cave is bigger than the last one," Niro said. "Find an exit, quickly!"

All five of them began searching for a crack in the bedrock, but it was hard to see the actual cave walls with all the sapphires growing on them. Desperate, Zerie began moving fast, using her talent to speed through the chamber, examining every inch of the rock walls.

"It's getting too tight," Tryan cried. "Marinell, be careful!"

An image of Marinell's tail filled Zerie's mind. Marinell's tail with a long scratch down the side from where she'd been caught by a crystal. Zerie shoved the image out of her mind and kept looking for a way out.

The pearl came into her mind.

She pushed it away.

It came back.

"I found it! Here!" Zerie cried. This opening was strange, an almost perfect circle barely bigger than she was. It was dark inside. She had no idea whether it would lead anywhere. But they were going to be cut to pieces if they stayed in the sapphire room. "Follow me."

She swam into the dark space, wishing for a lanternfish. "Light," she whispered. "I need light."

Softly, the pearl on her wrist began to glow. Zerie's eyes widened in surprise, but she didn't stop moving. She had to keep going so there would be room behind her for her friends. This tunnel was too narrow for her to even turn around in. "Are you all back there?" she called.

"We're here," Tryan's voice reached her.

Zerie felt a rush of relief, and then her mind once again filled with images of the blue pearl. *What is going on?* she wondered. *I'm the one using the pearl, but I don't think my emotions are as focused on it as the rest of theirs are.*

She held her arm out, trying to light the way in front of her. All she saw was the same reddish rock that the caves had been made up of—but this rock had circles carved into it, and it wound over her and under her and over her again. *Like a twister,* Zerie thought.

"This is it!" she cried. "This is the twisted tunnel!"

"Zerie, hurry. There are emeralds growing back here," Tryan said. "They're growing fast."

Zerie put on a burst of speed, realizing too late that she had accidentally slipped into using her talent. She'd left the others far behind. She stopped swimming, and immediately felt a rush of new, cool water around her.

There must be an opening somewhere behind me that is letting in water, Zerie realized as her body rose toward the top of the twisted tunnel. The space itself had grown wider. She suddenly understood what was happening.

"Everyone be careful!" she called. But she didn't know if they could hear her.

As she began to fall, she hoped desperately that the others would feel her fear and see an image of what was happening.

She was going over the Great Waterfall.

.17.

"Ned! What are you doing here?" Brink cried.

"I've been a prisoner here for days," Ned replied, staring through the iron bars. "I was on patrol with the Winged Monkeys, searching for you and Zerie and Vashti, when we were captured by Glinda's soldiers. But what are *you* doing here?"

"I—" Brink's words were cut short by a loud groaning sound, and suddenly the ground began to shake.

The Glass Cat took off running, vanishing into the darkness so quickly that she might as well have been Tabitha making herself disappear.

"What's going on?" Ned cried.

"I don't know." Brink sank back into the shadows,

trying to think of something—anything—he could make an illusion of to hide himself. The ground kept shaking, and the walls were vibrating, too, he realized. The strange, mournful groan continued, echoing through the stone hallways.

Is this Glinda's response to my escape? he wondered. If it was, she would be paying attention again, and so her protective enchantment would be back up. He wouldn't be able to hide.

As quickly as it had started, the shaking stopped. There was one last groan, and then the sound faded away, its diminishing echoes bouncing through the dungeons until it finally died out.

For a long moment, there was no sound at all. Brink found himself holding his breath.

Eventually he relaxed. Nobody seemed to be coming for him. He stood up and moved quickly back to Ned's cell.

"What's going on?" Ned demanded. "What was that?"

"I have no idea," Brink replied.

"You have to get us out of here," Ned said. "*Now.* We can talk when we're free."

"Us?" Brink asked.

"My squadron is in here, too." Ned frowned. "Somewhere."

"Do you mean Winged Monkeys? You want me to set Monkeys free?" Brink cried. "Those Monkeys chased me halfway through Oz. And so did you, by the way. Those Monkeys took Zerie and Vashti!"

"Brink." Ned's voice was more serious than Brink had ever heard it. "Find a way to get me out of here."

He's right, Brink thought, forcing himself to calm down. He couldn't leave his brother in a dungeon, no matter what Ned had done. They could yell at each other later. "Do you have any ideas?" he asked.

"The guardroom is at the top of the next staircase," said the Glass Cat, reappearing out of the shadows as if nothing had happened. "There is a master key in there."

"I'll be back," Brink told Ned, heading for the stairs. The cat trailed after him.

"The guard is bigger than you, and he has a spear," she said. "What are you going to do?"

Brink grinned at her. "Look in the mirror," he said.

When he reached the top of the stairs, he stopped and took a deep breath. If that shaking and groaning had been Glinda putting her enchantment back up, he wouldn't be able to do an illusion. He had no choice, though. He had to try.

Concentrating hard, he began the illusion. He was going to make himself look like a soldier again. To his surprise, it worked right away, and it felt as easy as putting on a hat. He didn't waste time thinking about it—he just hurried up the last step and went into the guardroom. "They want you down at the clockwork dungeon," he said, trying to sound official.

"Why?" asked the guard.

Brink just grunted in reply.

With a sigh, the guard tromped off down the stairs, leaving Brink on guard. As soon as the footsteps had died away, Brink grabbed the iron key that hung on the wall and ran back down to Ned. He unlocked the cell door and pulled it open, wincing as it gave a loud squeak.

Ned raised his fists, ready to fight.

"What are you doing?" Brink cried.

His brother frowned. "Brink?"

"Huh? Oh!" Brink dropped the illusion, and Ned gaped at him.

"Is that your talent?" Ned asked. "You disguise yourself?"

"I make illusions," Brink said. "And Zerie moves fast, and Vashti levitates. It's why you and your Monkey friends were chasing us, remember? So you could catch us and take away our magic?"

"Brink, don't be stupid." Ned snatched the key out of his hand and pushed past him out of the cell. He immediately began unlocking all the cells in the row, without even checking to see who was in them. "I'm in Glinda's dungeon," he went on as Brink followed him. "So are the Winged Monkeys, Ozma's own loyal soldiers. Doesn't that tell you that Glinda is against Ozma?"

"Yes, but I'm against Ozma, too," Brink insisted. "I'm against *you*."

Ned finally stopped and turned to look at him. "Brink, Ozma was trying to find people with magical talents so that they could help her. She knew a war was coming. She just didn't know who her enemy was."

Brink groaned in frustration. He didn't understand any of this. "Ozma sent Monkeys after me, and then Glinda locked me in a clockwork cell. As far as I can see, they're *both* bad."

Ned's face paled. "You were in the clockwork

dungeon? I heard terrible things about that. How did you escape?"

"I keep telling him that he *hasn't* escaped yet," the Glass Cat said, stalking down the corridor toward them. "We are still in Glinda's Palace. Until we're out of it, we're not safe."

"Is that the Glass Cat?" Ned said, awed. "Princess Ozma said the cat had been gone for years."

"I am right here," the cat snarled. "Don't talk about me as if I'm not."

"The Glass Cat disagreed with Ozma's ban on magic. Right?" Brink asked her.

The Glass Cat looked haughtily away and didn't answer.

"That magical ban was never true," Ned said. "If you had stayed with Princess Ozma, she probably would have told you. She missed you terribly."

The Glass Cat studied him, narrowing her beautiful emerald eyes. "*You* stayed with Ozma. I saw you in the magic mirror. You were there with Ozma and Vashti and Zerie."

"Where?" Ned asked, baffled.

"In the Emerald City. Then on an airship with Tabitha," the cat added. "Approaching this palace, ready to attack. So what are you doing here in the dungeons?"

Brink felt as if a cold hand was squeezing his heart. "Did your attack fail?" He wasn't even sure whose side he was supposed to be on in this battle, but he didn't want Glinda to strengthen her enchantment again. If she had won her battle, she might turn her attention back inward at any second.

Ned looked as confused as Brink felt. "No. I was never part of any attack. I was never on an airship with Tabitha—I mean, besides when I first took her to meet Ozma."

The Glass Cat arched her back, ready to spit at him. Ned backed away, his hands up in surrender. "I'm telling you the truth," he said evenly. "But I think I know what happened. Brink, the last time I saw you was in the Tilted Forest with Zerie and Vashti. You three ran so fast that you basically disappeared. That's when Glinda's soldiers ambushed us from below, and they brought us here."

"Did you see Glinda?" Brink asked.

"For a moment. They put me in a room with my hands bound. It was a clockwork workshop, and there was a clockwork man that looked half-done. One of her servants spent about an hour measuring me, and then Glinda came in, looked at me, and waved her wand."

The cat's back arched higher. "What then?"

"Then my face appeared on the clockwork man, and the soldiers dragged me away and put me in the dungeon."

Brink was stunned. Even the Glass Cat seemed surprised, and nothing ever rattled her. "So the person in Glinda's mirror, the one who is with Ozma and Tabitha . . . that's a clockwork man with your face?" Brink said slowly.

"A clockwork *spy*," the cat corrected him.

Ned's hands clenched into fists. "Princess Ozma trusted me. I was the only one—besides Tabitha—whom she told her suspicions to. The only one who knew that our true enemy was Glinda the Good."

"That makes you the perfect spy," the Glass Cat said. "This clockwork version of you must know all of Ozma's plans. Which means Ozma's plans are going to fail."

"But the attack must be happening. Glinda *is* distracted," Brink said. "Her protective enchantment is gone. I was able to use my talent easily just now."

Six Winged Monkeys had come out of the cells and gathered around Ned. The cat wrinkled her nose in disgust at their smell, and Brink couldn't help feeling frightened of them, but Ned simply turned and spoke to them. "We need to get out of this palace and warn Ozma. Split up and find an escape route if you can. Whoever reaches freedom first, head straight for the princess. Tell her that Ned is a spy."

The Monkeys looked quizzically at him.

"Ned is a spy," he repeated. "Move out!"

The Monkeys scattered.

"Now we need to go, as well." The cat shot Brink an exasperated look. "Will you finally follow me?"

She didn't wait for an answer, but simply took off running. Brink went after her, Ned right on his heels. Nobody spoke. They didn't want to get caught, but also the cat was moving so quickly that it was hard to keep up with her. There was no time for conversation.

Brink's head was spinning as he tried to follow her transparent glass tail, which whipped angrily back and forth as she wound her way down a back staircase away from the dungeon. He tried to make sense of what he'd just found out—that his brother, who had chased him through Oz on an airship, who had captured Tabitha and brought her to Ozma for punishment, who had betrayed him, was in fact on his side. That Ozma, the one they'd all been hiding their magical talents from for years, was their friend. That Tabitha and Vashti were with Ozma's army, and so they hadn't lost their talents after all.

But where was Zerie?

"It should be somewhere on this level," the Glass Cat said, slowing to a walk. She had taken them down several flights of stone stairs, and now they were in what looked like a row of storerooms. The hallway was dusty and deserted, and the rooms they passed were filled with shelves holding jars and bags of grain.

"What should be on this level?" Brink asked, whispering even though he didn't see any soldiers or servants.

"The secret door," the cat said, as if he should know that already.

Brink glanced at his brother. Ned shrugged.

"It is hidden on the outside by plants and trees, but on the inside I don't know," the cat said testily. Brink thought she was probably annoyed at herself for being ignorant about anything. The cat didn't like to admit weakness.

"If you don't know, what makes you think it's on this level?" Ned asked.

Brink shot him a look. The cat tended to be very rude when someone questioned her.

"This is the lowest level, isn't it?" she spat. "Where else would it be?"

Ned opened his mouth as if he might argue, so Brink jumped in to stop him. "You mean it's a door at the base of the palace? That's why it can be hidden by plants."

"Yes, it is in the foundation. It was placed there by the Wizard of Oz," the cat replied. "It is made of emerald." As they spoke, she wove her way into and out of various storerooms, passing food supplies, stocks of weapons, and a chamber filled with clock-work parts. Now that he knew what to look for, Brink began scanning the walls for a green door.

"If there's a door in one of these rooms, it wouldn't be much of a secret," Ned commented. "Is there a rea-son the Wizard hid it on the outside? Did he not care if it was hidden on the inside, too?"

"I don't presume to know the workings of the Wizard's mind," the cat replied. "Generally the think-ing of humans bores me, anyway. I simply know there's a door, because once I hunted a mouse that ran through it, and I followed it inside."

"Then you should know exactly where it is," Ned said. "You came through it!"

"I was paying attention to the mouse," she replied, her voice dripping with disdain. "And I left through the front gate."

"If it's disguised on the outside, it probably is in here, too," Brink guessed, ignoring them. "If I were going to hide something, I would put an illusion on it to make it look like something else."

"Well, how are we supposed to find it, then?" Ned asked tensely. "We could be looking at it right now and not know."

Brink stood still, thunderstruck. "I would know."

"What do you mean?" his brother asked.

"When Zerie and Vashti and I arrived at Glinda's Palace, there was a bridge across the raging river. A great, golden span."

"Right, but it's broken," Ned said. "It's always been broken. I've seen it from the airships many times. Glinda uses magic to repair it when she wants to use it, but every time her spell wears off, the bridge breaks again."

"No, it's the other way around," Brink told him. "The bridge is never broken. It's enchanted to *look* that way. When Glinda uses the bridge, she is forced to remove the illusion, or else anyone watching would see her walking in the air and realize that the bridge was being hidden by a spell."

"What does this have to do with our current situation?" the cat demanded.

"I saw the bridge. I saw that it was whole, not broken, but Zerie and Vashti didn't." Brink was troubled by the memory, because it was the last time he'd seen his friends. "I'm not sure why, but I could see right through the illusion. At the time, I thought it was because of my talent. I create illusions, so illusions don't work on me."

"You'd be able to see the secret door, even though we can't," Ned said.

Brink nodded. Pushing in front of the Glass Cat, he scanned the room for a door. Nothing. But he wasn't discouraged. He hurried into the next room. Nothing. And again. And again.

In the fifth storeroom, behind a large wooden barrel filled with cider, Brink's eye caught a flash of green. He moved closer, peering around the barrel until he

saw what it was: a small door, half the height of a typical door, made entirely of emerald. Even the handle
was emerald. The only part that wasn't was a round
window near the top.

Setting his shoulder against the barrel, Brink shoved
it out of the way.

"What do you see?" Ned asked, coming up behind
him.

"What do *you* see?" Brink countered.

"The wall," his brother replied. "The same pink
stone wall that's everywhere else in here."

Brink reached out and ran his fingers over the
emerald door. He hadn't been able to make Zerie
see the bridge. Could he make Ned see this? He concentrated on the illusion, trying to break it. He tried
to make himself see the wall, like Ned did. Nothing
worked. Whatever enchantment lay on the door was
too strong.

"This is a waste of time," the cat complained. "Is
there a door or not?"

"Yes. It's made of emerald, and there's a round
window," Brink said.

"Then for goodness' sake, open it," she ordered.

Brink knelt in front of the little door so he could

reach the handle. But with his hand on the cool, smooth green stone, he stopped. The window was made of clear glass. He could see right through it. "Didn't you say there were plants outside this door?"

"Yes," the cat replied. "Smelly pickleberry bushes."

Brink's heart sank. He didn't see bushes. He saw fish. "Something is wrong." He pressed his face against the window, trying to figure it out. "There are things floating out there . . . it looks like seaweed. And there are fish."

"Fish?" Ned's tone was baffled.

"Yes," Brink said. "We're underwater."

For a moment nobody spoke. Then the cat sat down, slowly, on her haunches. "I remember a visit I made with Ozma and Glinda, many years ago, to a queen who could sink her entire city into a lake. This was how she defended herself from any enemy who came near." She sounded stunned and worried, and that was frightening. The cat was never worried. "Glinda's Palace also sits in the midst of a body of water—not a lake like Queen Coo-ee-oh's, but a raging river."

"You think Glinda figured out how to do the same thing, to sink her palace in defense," Ned said. It wasn't a question. "It's not just here, at the base of the palace. It's the entire palace."

"That's why the protective enchantment is gone," Brink realized. "She doesn't need it now because we're underwater. No one can get to us."

"Correct," said the cat. "And we can't get out. We're trapped."

.18.

Zerie fell for what seemed like hours. The water around her roared as loud as thunder as it churned over the cliff above. She had time to realize that they had been underground inside a mountain, or what seemed like one from this side. The twisted tunnel wormed its way through the mountain, ending in the sheer cliff that dropped down to the flatlands where Glinda's Palace lay amidst the raging river. All the underground waters in the mountain converged at the end, forming the huge, powerful waterfall.

It's not the fall that will hurt me, she thought. *It's the landing.* The water at the bottom was churning from the force of all the water falling on top of it.

She would be battered and thrown about by the sheer violence of it.

Zerie knew just what to do, and she didn't need the pearl to help her. The instant her body hit the raging river, she swam. Fast. She was away from the waterfall and out of danger instantly. But she couldn't stop and rest. Her friends were coming behind her, and they wouldn't be able to swim away from the fall. They would be pummeled by the water.

Still moving with the speed of her talent, Zerie pulled up reeds from the riverbed, weaving them the way Vashti had taught her, moving so fast that she couldn't even see her fingers pulling the strands through and around and through one another again. She pictured the net being done . . . and it was done.

Zerie swam back toward the fall, her mind filling with images as the merpeople fell—images of confusion, of fear, and of the blue pearl. The merpeople were counting on the pearl to protect them, but Zerie didn't feel sure that it would. She only knew it would protect *her*.

She could tell from their feelings when they reached the bottom, with the heavy waterfall pounding on top of them. As they landed, she caught them in her net one by one and sped them safely away from the Great Waterfall.

Only when all the merpeople were in the relative calm of the river did she stop moving fast. She was exhausted.

"Zerie, are you all right?" Tryan asked, taking her hand. "You used a lot of power."

"I need to rest," she admitted. "But it's hard. The current is still so strong here. I'm fighting just to stay in place."

"Now that we're all here, we needn't stay in place," Marinell said. "The current will speed us toward the grotto beneath Glinda's Palace." She sounded tired, too, and Zerie realized that they were all worn out from the stress of trying to escape the crystal caves.

They floated for a few moments, letting the current pull them.

"Dive down," Princess Sirena finally said. "The raging river only rages at the top. This river runs deep, filling the grotto up ahead. We'll be more comfortable at the bottom."

The merpeople all dove, images of the pearl coming from them the whole time. Zerie dove after them, but she was confused. They were safe now—why was the pearl so obvious in their emotions? She was the one in danger—her timepiece read only twenty minutes left.

As she swam with them, she began to hear a buzzing sound. *Not a sound,* she corrected herself. *Thoughts.* Not from her friends, but somewhere else. A hundred thoughts at once, running through her head like buzzing bees. Zerie tried to shake it off, to focus on images. But there were more of those now, too, pictures entering her mind of pink stone walls, a large clockwork gear, golden doors, fighting Winged Monkeys, and soldiers.

"Glinda's Palace is near," she said. "I hear so many thoughts and feel so many emotions."

As she spoke, the riverbed fell away beneath her, dropping into an impossibly large underwater canyon. Marbled pink stone rose in spires from the bottom, far below, and pink lanternfish floated everywhere. It was Glinda's grotto.

"It can be overwhelming to be near a crowd," Tryan told her. "Try to focus on one thing, and it will help block out the noise."

Zerie nodded. She knew what to focus on: the pearl. It was what the merpeople had been focused on for most of the past day, and she wasn't sure why. She brought it up in her mind and allowed all the other images to come to her: Marinell's images of the pearl, always glowing; Niro's images of it, lashed to Zerie's wrist in the strands of her bracelet; Tryan's images of the pearl, which always included Zerie herself; Princess Sirena's images of the pearl, in a crown on her head.

Zerie stopped short, stunned. But the image remained—her pearl, large and blue and beautiful, as the centerpiece in an elaborate crown on Sirena's long, thick, silver-blue hair.

"That's right, dirt girl!" the princess snarled. She grabbed Zerie's wrist with strong fingers and jerked the bracelet so hard that it broke. "This is *my* pearl!"

Zerie was too shocked to even fight back. The pearl was gone, off her wrist and in Princess Sirena's grasp.

"The three Pearls of Power belonged to the people of Aquaria," the princess spat. "Pearls come from the sea, and they belong to the sea. They were stolen many years ago by Ozma's ally, Prince Inga. But they were never his, and they were never hers. They are mine."

Zerie struggled to make sense of what was

happening. Suddenly the images coming from the merpeople had stopped entirely. They had taken up positions around Princess Sirena and were watching Zerie with cold eyes.

"You . . . you never had any intention of helping us," Zerie said. "You lied to Ozma."

"I didn't care if we reached Glinda's Palace," Princess Sirena replied. "That was not my goal. I simply agreed to Ozma's request because I saw an opportunity to reclaim one of my people's lost treasures."

"But the Nome King," Zerie cried. "You've seen his work! He's invading Aquaria as well as Oz!"

"Yes. That troubled me," the princess said. "But I am not worried, because now that I have the pearl, it will protect Aquaria from harm."

"I don't think it works like that," Zerie began, but Sirena cut her off.

"Don't tell me about the magic of my own treasure," she snapped.

Zerie felt anger rise up through her confusion. How dare the merpeople betray her like this? Betraying Oz was one thing. But they had traveled with Zerie. They had become friends with her. She had rescued them from danger during the colorca attack, and the poppies, and the Great Waterfall. And yet they were turning on her!

"Why didn't you take it earlier, then?" she demanded. "Why go through this whole charade?"

"There is more power in the pearl if it is given willingly," Princess Sirena replied. "I hoped you would be convinced to join us, and then I could ask you for the pearl as a way to protect us all, your own people. You loved being a mermaid. If you became one of us, you would want to do what was best for us."

Zerie studied the faces of her friends, understanding now that all the beautiful images they'd shown her weren't their true feelings. They'd been trying to draw her in, to convince her to stay with them. Even Tryan, who had been her closest friend, who had kissed her cheek in the poppy pod. He'd been lying all along.

"Not always. You *would* make a beautiful mermaid," he said softly.

Zerie couldn't believe him. Did he think flattery would make her forgive him?

Her thoughts were suddenly so much clearer than they'd been for days. Why had Zerie thought she was attracted to Tryan? She didn't even know him. It was Brink who Zerie cared about, Brink who needed her.

Zerie turned her back on them, ready to follow the throng of voices to Glinda's Palace. Then she hesitated.

"That pearl won't protect you the way you think it will," she told Princess Sirena, turning back. "It's not like a suit of armor that just keeps bad things from happening. You have to learn how to use it, and I'm not even sure it will protect more than one person. Especially since it wasn't given willingly."

"The pearl will recognize its rightful owner and work for me," Princess Sirena said haughtily. "I represent the people of Aquaria, so if it protects me, it protects them."

Right at that moment, the water behind Princess Sirena moved all at once, and suddenly a terrifying mouth opened near her head, two rows of knifelike teeth on display.

"Look out!" Zerie yelled.

At the last second, Niro shoved the colorca aside. But while doing so, his shoulder hit Princess Sirena's arm, and the bracelet with the blue pearl fell from her hand.

"The pearl!" she cried.

But there was no time to go after it. The colorca

had returned to attack again, and there were at least two more with it. They changed their appearance as they moved, going from pink like the stone of the grotto to the slate gray of the water, but their mouths always showed, their terrifying teeth snapping viciously at the merpeople.

Niro, Tryan, and Marinell whipped out their tridents and began to fight the dangerous beasts, while Princess Sirena attempted to dive after the pearl. A colorca attacked from below, teeth grazing her arm, and she screamed. Niro grabbed her and pulled her away.

The bracelet vanished into the depths.

Zerie felt frozen in place. The colorcas must have followed them, hidden by their camouflage, waiting until they sensed that the merpeople were vulnerable. As soon as the pearl had changed hands, any magical protection it had offered was gone.

And now the pearl itself was gone.

"Zerie, *go!*" Tryan sped toward her, stabbing at a colorca as he did. "You're almost out of time."

He grabbed her hand and swam, pulling her after him.

"I don't need you to save me," she snapped.

"You've saved me before," Tryan retorted. "Use

your talent. Make us faster. You don't have time to waste."

Zerie realized that he wasn't swimming away from the colorcas as much as he was swimming toward something else—a large shadow on the floor of the grotto. The roar of thoughts and images came from that shadow.

"Glinda's Palace!" she gasped. "It's underwater."

"Use your talent," he repeated. "There's a colorca chasing us."

Zerie felt a stab of guilt. "I should help the others. They wouldn't have escaped the colorcas last time without my talent."

"No, Zerie." For a brief moment she saw an image from him again—her golden timepiece. "You don't have time to help."

Still, Zerie hesitated. She was angry with the mer-people, but she couldn't leave them to the colorcas. Not even if it meant she ran out of time and was forced to remain a mermaid herself.

"That was another lie," Tryan said. "Sirena wanted you to think you'd be one of us so you would hand over the pearl. You won't, Zerie. When time runs out, you'll be a human again. You'll drown."

Zerie stared at him, horrified.

The colorca's mouth appeared, snapping at him, and Tryan stabbed at it, shoving it away with his trident. Then he turned back to her, his gray-blue eyes desperate. "Please, Zerie, move fast!"

So she did. She pictured that shadow on the floor of the grotto getting closer and closer until it looked like the enormous pink and gold palace she had seen four days earlier. And then she was there.

Only at that moment did she realize the problem: she was supposed to find the hidden door that the Wizard had placed at the base of the palace, let herself inside, sneak through, and then open the outer doors for Ozma's army.

But the palace was entirely underwater.

Even if she could still open the hidden emerald door, she wouldn't be able to let Ozma in because Ozma was on land.

Zerie hesitated, unsure what to do now. She swam to the door, its green stone easy to spot against the pink marble of the rest of the castle. It was a small door with a round window. If she opened it, would it flood the palace? *Could* she open it against the pressure of the water?

A stabbing pain shot through her tail. Zerie spun around, looking around wildly for camouflaged col-orcas. The pain came again, even though no mouth full of sharp teeth appeared. Her chest began to ache.

She realized what was happening. Her time had run out. She was becoming human again. And she was deep underwater.

.19.

"It must have been when we heard that noise and felt the shaking. That must be when Glinda sank the palace," Ned said. He sighed. "None of the Winged Monkeys would have been able to escape. We've been underwater the whole time."

"Ozma doesn't know that she has a spy in her midst," Brink added.

Ned nodded grimly. "We have to find another way out. We'll go to the top, to the highest tower. Maybe we can swim from there."

"The important thing about the raging river is that it's raging," the Glass Cat replied. "Not even the strongest swimmers would be able to survive."

"There's not much choice," Brink told her. "We can't escape through this door."

He kicked at the emerald door, and it exploded inward, turning to dust.

The force of the water rushing in knocked Brink off his feet. Ned fell backward, pushed by a wave of river water. The Glass Cat sped out of sight, running as fast as she could.

Sputtering to breathe and with his heart hammering in his chest, Brink fought his way to his feet. The emerald door was gone, along with about three feet of the wall. Water poured through the hole at a terrifying rate.

And Zerie Greenapple lay on the floor in front of him, gasping for air.

"Zerie!" Brink cried.

"She's hurt, pick her up," Ned said quickly. "We have to get out of here."

Brink scooped Zerie up and waded through the storeroom. The water was already up to his knees. As soon as he got into the hallway, Ned pulled the door shut, trapping the rushing water inside.

Brink put Zerie down. Panting and astonished, they all stared at one another.

"This door won't hold for long," Ned said after a few seconds. "We have to get to a higher floor."

"Can you walk?" Brink asked Zerie.

She blinked at him, her mouth hanging open in shock. He almost laughed. He knew exactly how she felt—absolutely baffled, but also absolutely happy. Still, they had to move. He knelt next to her on the floor.

"Zerie," he said. "Are you all right?"

"Yes," she finally said. "Are you?"

"Well, I'm not the one who just burst through a stone wall from deep underwater," he pointed out.

"But you're a prisoner." She frowned. "Aren't you? Ned, is the battle over? How did you get here when the palace is underwater? I was supposed to let you in."

Now Ned looked confused.

"Did you sneak in to rescue Brink?" Zerie asked.

A loud crash came from the other side of the door. The water was pushing the big cider barrels around, throwing them against the walls.

"We can't talk now. We have to move," Brink insisted.

"Oh. I'm sorry. I had no time to open the door, I

had to use my power to age the rock into sand so I could get in." Zerie climbed to her feet. "I'm fine," she told Brink as he reached to help her. "Join hands."

Ned opened his mouth to ask why, but Brink already knew. He grabbed his brother's hand, and then he took Zerie's hand. For a brief moment he let himself enjoy the sensation of her skin against his. Zerie smiled and squeezed his hand.

Then they were running. So fast that the doors and walls went by in a blur, and four flights of stone stairs did, as well. Flashes of faces sped by—Glinda's uniformed soldiers and escaped prisoners and Winged Monkeys. Brink tried to move his feet, but it was hard. When Zerie used her talent, he usually just held on and hoped he didn't bang into anything.

She stopped in a wide hall made of pink marble. Brink tried to catch his breath. Ned looked stunned.

"Zerie's talent is to speed things up," Brink told him. "Obviously."

Ned nodded wordlessly.

"Ned knows what my talent is," Zerie said. "Now tell me what happened. Ned, where's Tabitha?"

"She is on the road of yellow brick with the Winged Monkeys, wondering how to attack Glinda now that

heart beginning to calm down. Tryan was holding her, his tail keeping them in place as the river raged around them.

"Yes. I wanted to be sure you had made it in time. I never wanted you to get hurt," he said.

"What about the colorcas?" Zerie asked. "Are the others all right?"

"We fought off the attack. Niro's arm is wounded," Tryan told her. "I asked them to come with me to see if you needed help, but Princess Sirena has them searching the grotto instead, looking for the pearl."

Zerie shook her head. "The Nome King is a danger to your people as well as the people of Oz," she said. "Sirena should be helping Ozma, not worrying about a treasure."

"I agree," he said. "But that's not my choice."

Zerie sighed. "It's too bad. I could use the help of the merpeople right now. I need to find the mechanism at the bottom of Glinda's Palace. If I can age the metal and make it rot away, my friend Vashti may be able to raise the castle back to land. Then Ozma's army can fight Glinda."

"Is that why you came back out of the palace?"

"Yes. I thought I could move quickly enough that I

wouldn't run out of air. But the current is too strong for me without a tail," she replied sadly.

"You don't have Princess Sirena's help," Tryan said. "But you have mine. I will swim down and find the mechanism with you. You can move us fast, and I can hold you against the raging river."

"You'd do that for me?"

"Of course. I do care about you, Zerie," he said. "You and I are friends."

She smiled. "Thank you."

"Are you ready?" Tryan asked.

"Yes." Zerie took a deep breath, he wrapped his arms around her waist, and they dove. Tryan swam as only a merperson could, strong against the current. Zerie used her talent to speed them through the water.

At the base of the palace were two gigantic metal clamps, one on each side of the massive building. Zerie focused on the closest one, picturing the metal as the waters rushed around it, wearing it away, turning it to rust, the rust spreading and spreading until the entire clamp had disappeared.

It was done.

Zerie felt like her chest might explode. She turned

to Tryan, wishing she could still communicate with her mind. He gave a mighty kick and sped them back up to the surface.

As Zerie filled her lungs with air, Tryan chuckled. "I *can* still read your thoughts," he said. "You just can't read mine."

Zerie smiled. "Then you know I'm thinking that we have to go back down and rust away the second clamp."

He nodded.

She took another breath, and they sped back to the bottom of the grotto. Glinda's Palace was beginning to shift in the water now, with only one clamp holding it down. Zerie went to work on the remaining clamp, hoping that her friends in the castle were still safe with it moving around so much.

And hoping that Vashti would know what to do when Zerie was finished.

The second clamp rusted into nothingness, setting the building free in the water.

Tryan pulled Zerie away from it, rushing back up to the surface of the river so she could breathe. Zerie held on to him. There was nothing more she could do now.

For a moment, nothing happened. The river raged. The golden bridge arched over the river, broken in the middle. From her spot in the water, Zerie could see flags and spears and horses on the road of yellow brick—Ozma's army.

Then suddenly a pink tower broke the surface of the water, followed by another, shorter one, and then by the entire castle itself. Glinda's Palace, pink and gold, emerged from the raging stream, floating like a hot air balloon. Up, up, up it went, until the pink rock foundation appeared, water pouring from the hole Zerie had made.

The palace drifted toward the road of yellow brick and landed gently on the ground.

"Is Glinda still in there?" Tryan asked.

"I don't know," Zerie said.

She held her breath, watching. Ozma's horseback soldiers galloped toward the palace, forming a ring around it, their shining spears pointed at the enormous golden gates.

With a metallic clang, the gates swung open . . . and Brink Springer appeared, carrying the Glass Cat. Ned came out behind him, followed by a squadron of Winged Monkeys.

Zerie felt a rush of relief. It was over. Her friends were all right.

Ozma's soldiers rushed into the palace while the Glass Cat leaped from Brink's arms with a look of distaste on her face. She saw Vashti and Tabitha run forward to greet the Springer brothers.

"I guess I should head back to Princess Sirena now," Tryan said.

Zerie nodded. "I hope you find the blue pearl."

"You do?" he asked, surprised.

"It seems important to Sirena. Keeping Oz safe is more important to me than a pearl. Friendship is more important." Zerie shrugged. "If your princess doesn't care about any of that, then I hope she finds what she does care about."

Tryan studied her face. "You are a good person," he said.

"And you're a good merperson," she told him. They laughed.

"I'll help you to shore. You can't swim in this river," Tryan said. With two kicks of his mighty tail, they were at the riverbank.

"Zerie!" Brink cried, running over. "Thank goodness. We had no idea what happened to you."

"Goodbye, Zerie Greenapple," Tryan said.

"Goodbye," she replied.

Brink reached down, and she clasped his hand. By the time he'd pulled her out of the raging river, Tryan was gone.

"Was that a merman?" Brink asked.

"Yes, my friend Tryan," she told him.

Brink looked as if he wanted to ask more, but he didn't get the chance. There was a loud trumpeting sound, and the captain of Ozma's army rode out of the golden gates. "We've searched the palace. There is no sign of Glinda the sorceress," he announced. "And her soldiers have surrendered."

"Let's go." Brink took Zerie's hand and led her over to where Princess Ozma sat on a beautiful green horse fitted with a golden saddle. Ozma cradled the Glass Cat in her arms, and the cat was purring.

"I didn't know she could do that," Zerie said.

Princess Ozma smiled. "My dear friend the Glass Cat and I have resolved our misunderstanding," she said. "She realizes that my ban on magic was never truly meant to prevent the people of Oz from having talents. And now, with Glinda's defeat, I declare the ban officially lifted!"

A cheer went up from the soldiers and the Winged Monkeys.

Vashti came running and threw her arms around Zerie, followed by Tabitha. "We were so worried about you!" Vashti cried.

"It was a strange experience, being a mermaid," Zerie admitted. "Vashti, I can't believe you levitated an entire castle!"

"I could never do that on my own. The green pearl gave me amazing strength," Vashti said.

"And your pearl made you very wise," Zerie said, turning to Tabitha. "You figured out this whole plan, didn't you?"

Tabitha made a face. "I wouldn't have realized that Ned was a spy if not for the pearl," she admitted. "I was too busy having a crush on him to notice that he wasn't behaving exactly like himself." She took Ned's hand—the real Ned. "But when I learned to let the pearl help me, it was as if someone had taken a blindfold off and I saw right away that Ned was a clockwork man."

"That reminds me, I must remove the enchantment from that machine," Princess Ozma said. "Bring me the spy!"

"He's gone limp, your highness," one of the soldiers reported. Ned's face was gone from the clockwork figure. It was just a lifeless machine now.

Ozma's smooth forehead creased with worry. "Then Glinda has ended the enchantment."

"Does that mean . . . She isn't dead, is she?" Zerie asked.

"No, she cannot die," Ozma assured her. "But she has vanished, and who knows where she's gone."

"To the Nome King, most likely," Tabitha said. "This war may not be over yet."

"Only time will tell," Princess Ozma agreed gravely. Then she smiled. "But today we celebrate. It's a wonderful thing that I found you all to help me. This was your victory. You put all your talents together and brought down our enemy."

Zerie, Vashti, and Tabitha shared a smile. "That's because friends are strongest together," Zerie said. "Even when we aren't actually together!"

"Let us return to the Emerald City," the princess suggested. "I will send the Wizard here with his builders to repair this palace."

"Come in the airship with Tabitha and me," Ned told Brink. "We all have a lot of explaining to do."

Brink nodded, and they started toward one of the airships. "It's hard to believe we're going to travel with the Winged Monkeys on purpose," Zerie commented. "We spent so long running from them."

"And the magic ban is lifted." Brink squeezed her hand. "We won't have to sneak out to the woods anymore to practice our talents. I'll miss that."

"We still can if you want to," Zerie told him.

Brink stopped walking, turned toward her, and kissed her on the cheek. "Definitely," he said.

Laura J. Burns

Laura J. Burns has written more than thirty books for kids and teens, touching on topics from imaginary lake monsters to out-of-control Hollywood starlets. She has also written for the TV shows *Roswell*, *1-800-MISSING,* and *The Dead Zone*. Laura lives in New York with her husband, her kids, and her two exceptionally silly dogs.